“Time To Pay Up, Angel,”

Drew whispered into her ear.

Anticipation tightened the breath in her throat. “What are you talking about?”

“You want me to kiss you. I can see it in your eyes.”

“No! How dare you—”

“Yes, I dare,” he murmured, parting her hair and pressing his lips against the back of her neck. “I’ve dared to admit what you keep trying to deny.”

“I don’t know what you’re talking about,” she said breathlessly, tipping her head forward as his lips slid along her nape.

“Then let me spell it out for you.” His voice thrummed in her ear, sending hot shivers along her skin. “I still want you. Just as much as I ever did. Maybe more.”

Dear Reader,

Happy New Year! And what a *fabulous* year it's going to be. First, due to *overwhelming* popular demand, we have another fun-filled lineup of *Man of the Month* books . . . starting with *Lyon's Cub* by Joan Hohl. In the future, look for *Man of the Month* stories by some of your favorite authors, including Diana Palmer, Ann Major, Annette Broadrick and Dixie Browning.

But Silhouette Desire is not only just *Man of the Month,* because each and every month we bring you six sensuous, scintillating, love stories by six terrific writers. In January, we have Jackie Merritt, Amanda Stevens (this is her long-awaited sequel to *Love is a Stranger* and it's called *Angels Don't Cry*), Kelly Jamison, Cathie Linz and Shawna Delacorte.

And in February we're presenting a special promotion just in time for Valentine's Day called *Mystery Mates.* Read and see how each Bachelorette opens the door to love and meets the Bachelor of her dreams. This promotion is so wonderful, we decided to give you six portraits of the heroes, so you can see each man up close and *very* personal.

Believe it or not, that's just what I have in store for you the first *two months* of 1993—there's so much more to come! So keep reading, enjoying and letting me know how you feel.

All the best,

Lucia Macro
Senior Editor

AMANDA STEVENS

ANGELS DON'T CRY

Published by Silhouette Books New York
America's Publisher of Contemporary Romance

SILHOUETTE BOOKS
300 East 42nd St., New York, N.Y. 10017

ANGELS DON'T CRY

ISBN: 0-373-05758-X

First Silhouette Books printing January 1993

Printed in the U.S.A.

Books by Amanda Stevens

Silhouette Desire

Love is a Stranger #647
Angels Don't Cry #758

Silhouette Intimate Moments

Killing Moon #159
The Dreaming #199

AMANDA STEVENS

knew at an early age she wanted to be a writer and began her first novel at the age of thirteen. While majoring in English at Houston Community College and the University of Houston, she was encouraged to write a romance novel by one of her instructors, who was himself writing a historical. Her first romance was sold to Silhouette Intimate Moments in 1985. Amanda lives in Houston, Texas, with her husband of sixteen years and their five-year-old twins.

This book is gratefully dedicated to Margie Bullard and Jeanie Goad, who are not only my sisters but also my friends.

And to all the folks in Bradford, Arkansas—my hometown—for their generous support.

Prologue

Someone was calling to her, whispering her name softly, like the wind sighing through the trees.

Angel! Angel!

Ann Lowell moaned softly, her head moving from side to side on the pillow. Images danced through her unconscious—dark, threatening visions of a sky lit with lightning, of water deep and cold and black as it closed over her head, of blinding, numbing terror—

With a gasp Ann sprang upright in bed, her eyes staring blindly into the shadowed recesses of her bedroom. Her heart seemed to stop for a moment, then slammed against her chest in rapid, painful beats, temporarily driving away the memory of what had awakened her.

The storm, she thought weakly as she sagged back against the pillow, dazed and shaken. But...what storm? Moonbeams softly drenched her bedroom. The night sky outside her window was clear and starry.

A dream then—

No, not a dream. A *feeling*. A premonition. Her twin sister was in trouble. The revelation came to Ann quickly, startling her into alertness. She could sense the fear, could almost smell it. It was all around her, chilling her like a winter mist, settling over her like a dark and heavy shroud.

Something had happened to Aiden. Ann knew it as surely as she knew herself to be safe and sound in her own bedroom. She closed her eyes tightly, letting the sensations wash over her. The pulsing terror of her dream had given way to a strange calmness. Ann could feel herself sinking into a dangerous lethargy, a dark serenity that lulled and beckoned as though she were being pulled into a deep and dreamless sleep. Through it all came an unbearable sense of sorrow and loneliness...and betrayal. Strong, tearing emotions that for one brief moment were almost tangible. And then they began to fade....

"Aiden!" Ann screamed her sister's name aloud as she bolted upright in bed. Again and again she sought to capture the elusive link with her twin, sought until sweat broke hot on her skin, until her knuckles whitened where she clutched the quilt ever tighter, until she knew with certainty it was too late to say *I forgive you*.

"Oh, God." With shaking hands, she shoved aside the cover, reaching automatically for the telephone before she realized there was no one to call. Aiden and Drew had been divorced for a long time. Whether they kept in touch or not, Ann had no way of knowing. At any rate, she was not the one to call Drew Maitland.

She glanced at the bedside clock. Midnight. Midnight, and she had no idea where her sister was. Rising from her bed, she belted a robe around her as she walked to the window, staring blindly down at the garden.

She waited.

Her vigil at the window continued until the first lavender light of dawn stained the eastern sky, until the weak, winter sun broke through the horizon. Until nothing remained of the night before except memories. Still, she watched and she waited.

But the call from Cozumel, Mexico, did not come until two days later.

Her sister was dead.

One

Six months later.

Like its sleek, graceful namesake, Drew Maitland's dark green Jaguar prowled the quaint, narrow streets of Crossfield, Texas, with a careful, almost contemptuous observance of the posted speed limit. A traffic light turned red, and the car lunged to a halt, the powerful engine idling and thrumming impatiently. Tinted windows obscured the driver from curious, prying eyes, but the anonymity was only an illusion. Already the news had spread.

Peering between parted curtains at her front window, Wilma Gates hurriedly dialed the number of the house next door. Bernice Ballard answered on the first ring.

"You'll never guess who that car belongs to," Wilma challenged by way of greeting.

"Humph. Looks like one of those foreign jobs," Bernice noted in disapproval. "Probably one of those hotshots from the development company that's been nosing around here. They all act like they've got money to burn—"

"He's with Riverside Development Company all right, but you're never going to believe—"

"—I swear, the way they breeze into town, acting like they already own the place, making offers right and left for river-fronted property, telling us what we should do with *our* town—"

"It's that Maitland boy!" Wilma practically shouted, trying to recapture control of the conversation.

"—Not that I've got anything against progress, mind you, but I just think— *Who!*"

"You remember Drew Maitland, don't you?" Wilma asked smugly, noting the silence on the other end with immense satisfaction.

Bernice finally found her breath again. "*Well!* I never thought that boy would have the nerve to show his face in this town again."

"Nerve was one thing Drew Maitland was never short on," Wilma remarked dryly. "Remember all those pranks he used to pull, instigating all those wild parties down by the river? Not to mention what he did to Ann Lowell and her sister. Although I can't say Aiden's part in that whole sordid mess surprised me any. I don't mean to speak ill of the dead, but she always was a wild one. Ann was so sweet and courteous. It was such a shame, her having to leave town like that."

"Well, it seems mighty peculiar to me, that company sending *him* down here to do their business. Ann's property is one of the pieces they've been trying to buy for months. I can't imagine she'd want to do business with Drew Maitland. I know ten years is a long time, but people around here don't forget things. There's still talk about what he did—"

"People love to talk, you know that." Wilma pushed her face closer to the window as she strained to catch a last glimpse of the green car as it swooshed through the intersection. "Nothing Drew Maitland does should surprise anyone here in Crossfield anymore. I declare, when he walked into that church at Aiden's memorial service, I half expected the roof to collapse."

"Oh, I know," Bernice agreed piously. "But to give the devil his due, he did sit in the back and he left before the service was over. At least he spared poor Ann that much. I don't think she even knew he was there until I—well, I happened to mention to her at the cemetery that I thought it was him. Poor little thing turned pale as anything. I thought she was going to pass out cold—"

"And who could blame her, a shock like that—"

"Wilma! He's turning left down River Road. You don't suppose he's actually going out to the farm? Surely even he wouldn't have that kind of gall—"

"Call Gail! If he's going to the farm, he'll have to pass by her house..."

Ann stood under the dappled shade of one of the giant black locust trees lining the sidewalk of the Crossfield, Texas, city hall. She was late, but she couldn't seem to muster the courage needed to close the distance between herself and the crowd milling about outside the arched loggia as they waited for the town meeting to begin.

The breeze shifted, stirring the branches overhead and loosening a shower of tiny, white blossoms from the fragrant clusters. The heady scent filled her with nostalgia for long, lazy summer days, for moon-drenched nights by the river, for a time when she had been young and innocent and head over heels in love.

She shook her head slightly, trying to dispel the feeling, but ever since her cousin had called her at the university that morning with the news, Ann's mind had refused to register anything but all those elusive memories and those two, fateful words. "Drew's back."

All day, in anticipation of seeing him at this meeting tonight, Ann had tried to prepare herself. "It doesn't matter," she reminded herself over and over again. "It's been ten years. Nothing lasts that long. Except maybe hate." *Or love.* Luckily she felt neither of those emotions for Drew Maitland anymore. What she felt for him now, and for what he was trying to do to her town, was contempt.

How like him to imagine he could waltz back into Crossfield after all these years and change everything to suit his needs, his own self-serving ambition. She'd once been almost destroyed by his selfishness, but not this time. This time, she wouldn't run away. He didn't know it yet, but Drew Maitland was in for the fight of his life.

Bracing her shoulders with renewed determination, Ann crossed the lawn to the sidewalk leading up to the white stucco building. The excited chatter of the crowd filled the air like a swarm of angry bumblebees. Ann had never before seen such an enthusiastic turnout for a town meeting. But then, Crossfield had never before been threatened by a big city developer, she reminded herself grimly.

"Ann! Over here!"

Ann looked up to see Viola Pickles, president of the local Historical Society, waving a picket sign as she bore down upon Ann with resolve. Every time Ann saw Viola, she wondered if the little woman's sour disposition was the result of her forty years as a junior high school teacher or a self-fulfilling prophesy of her name. Ann was only too aware of the impact and expectations a name could elicit. For that very reason, she'd changed hers a long time ago.

"Ann, I need to talk to you before the meeting," Viola said urgently, clamping down on Ann's arm with surprising vigor. "Have you heard about the representative Riverside Development has sent down here?"

"Yes, I heard," Ann replied curtly, extricating herself from the clawlike grasp as she continued toward the steps, ever mindful of the curious stares, the whispered comments behind hands.

Viola blinked once behind the large, black-rimmed glasses she wore as she struggled to keep pace with Ann. "You already know about Drew Maitland?" There was a faint note of disappointment in her tone.

"Jack called me this morning between classes. Now, if you'll excuse me, Viola, I really do have to run—" Ann started up the steps with the older woman trailing her like a lost puppy.

"This isn't going to change your position, I hope." Viola's voice rose in corresponding increments as Ann's longer legs widened the distance between them. "There're a lot of people counting on you to represent us. We don't want Crossfield razed to make room for shopping malls and condos! You tell them that, Ann!" Viola called after her as Ann opened the glass door and stepped inside the air-conditioned corridor.

Her high heels clicked against the black and white mosaic tile floor as she hurried across the lobby to the council chambers, pausing outside the door for a moment to take a deep breath.

Go on, open the door. she commanded herself. *Get it over with. You'll probably find he's nothing like you remembered. You won't feel a thing.*

"Famous last words," she muttered as she reached for the knob and turned it. She opened the door, stepped inside, and stopped, her eyes sweeping the room with one frantic glance.

The blood pounded in her ears. Her stomach gave a violent quiver. Her knees began to tremble as a powerful relief flooded through her. *He isn't there.* It had all been a mistake. Drew hadn't come back.

"Ann! Over here! We're saving you a seat!" At the sound of her name being called, Ann stepped into the large room where dozens of folding chairs had been set up for the town meeting. The Historical Society had grouped themselves toward the front of the room, and several of the matrons were emphatically motioning her to join them as they zealously brandished placards with messages ranging from NO BULLDOZING IN CROSSFIELD to simply RIVERSIDE DEVELOPMENT GO HOME.

With a reluctant sigh Ann started toward them, noting that the only vacant chair left in the whole room was smack in the middle of their group between Bernice Ballard and Wilma Gates, who were staring at her with avid curiosity. Like a horde of locusts, they descended on her as soon as she sat down, stinging her with questions from every side.

"Have you seen him yet?"

"What's he like now?"

"What did he have to say for himself?"

"What's he look like?"

Before Ann could open her mouth to answer, the side door opened into the council chambers. Mayor Sikes walked into the room, followed by Drew Maitland, and the entire Historical Society took a collective breath.

"Drew..." His name slipped through Ann's lips on her own suspended breath as a thousand memories—images from a lifetime ago—cascaded through her. Stolen moments by the river, forbidden longings during hot, sleepless nights. And love, so powerful and enduring that it hadn't gone away...even after he'd married her sister.

Oh, God, why now? Ann thought desperately. Why now, when he was ten years too late? Why now, when all that was left between them were the memories? And Aiden. Always Aiden. She was almost a physical presence in the room with them, reminding Ann anew that this man had broken both their hearts.

Wilma Gates found her voice first. "Oh, Lord, he's still a handsome devil," she said reverently, smoothing back a wisp of her bluish gray hair. "And still wild as the wind, I don't doubt."

"Girls, we'll have our work cut out for us opposing him," Bernice predicted, her seventy-year-old eyes snapping with excitement. "That boy could charm the bloomers right off a virgin, I'll wager."

Ann's face flamed at that particular observation, her mind flying back to one moonlit night on the bank of the river, a night when she'd been lying in Drew's arms, their clothes strewn in the grass around them. She had stopped him, of course, before they'd gone too far. After getting dressed, Drew had held her in his arms again, telling her it was all right, that he'd wait for her until she was ready.

He hadn't waited, though, Ann thought bitterly. In the end, he hadn't waited for her.

She watched him walk through the room, stopping to talk with old friends and acquaintances, shaking hands and smiling, his dress and demeanor both elegantly understated. Her gaze slipped over him taking in with reluctant precision the beautiful cut of his gray, double-breasted suit, the stark white of his shirt splashed with the silk brilliance of his tie.

Older, perhaps a bit harsher-looking than she remembered, Drew Maitland was still the most compelling man she'd ever known. His eyes were as blue as the summer sky, and his light brown hair was still thick and sun-streaked and made for a woman's fingers.

What riveted her attention most, though, was the air of total self-confidence, which she remembered only too well. As an adolescent full of insecurities and self-doubts, she'd been drawn to him for his inner strength and confidence as surely as she'd been attracted to his astonishing good looks.

The combination was still just as devastating, she thought with a warning quiver in the pit of her stomach. And still just as dangerous.

Beside him, Crossfield's short, rotund mayor strutted and blustered with self-importance, looking like nothing so much as a bantam rooster in a coop full of hens as he back-clapped and smiled his way through the crowd. The comparison was inevitable, and Mayor Sikes fell short in more than just stature.

Completely undaunted, however, the mayor stepped to the podium and briskly rapped his gavel against the scarred wooden top as he called the meeting to order. There was a last-minute scramble as the stragglers from outside dashed in, and then the shuffling of feet and the low rumble of voices reluctantly faded away as everyone turned with anxious, expectant expressions to face the front of the room.

For good measure Mayor Sikes cleared his throat a couple of times as he surveyed the room over a pair of antiquated bifocals perched on the end of his nose. "Folks, we're going to go ahead and get started here. As most of you already know, a company called Riverside Development has shown a great deal of interest in our community of late..."

As the mayor rambled on, Ann shifted restlessly against the cold back of the metal chair. Unconsciously she crossed her legs as she fervently tried to keep her eyes focused straight ahead. To avert her gaze even fractionally would bring Drew into her line of vision, and every time she looked at him, her heart seemed to stop.

"...I know we're all anxious to hear the latest word from Riverside," the gravelly, grating voice droned on. "But first, there are one or two other matters of business we need to address. Last month Bernice Ballard requested the addition of a Stop sign at the corner of Elm and Pecan. The council and I have taken that request under serious consideration..."

As the mayor's voice droned relentlessly on, Drew found his attention straying. Not far. Just a few feet away, where Angel Lowell sat rigidly facing the front of the room, apparently absorbed in every word being spoken. An ironic smile touched his lips as he noticed the legion of women surrounding her and the protest signs they were holding.

It had been his idea to come to Crossfield to try to smooth the way for the multimillion dollar project Riverside Development had in mind. For months now, since they'd gone public with their plans, Riverside had met with steady opposition from a number of Crossfield citizens and property owners in the area. As vice president of public relations for the huge conglomerate that owned Riverside Development, Drew had seemed the perfect choice to deal with the lingering antagonism his company had generated. After all, he'd grown up here, and even with his cloudy past, he had a better chance of gaining their trust and support than an outsider would.

But at that time he hadn't realized his antithesis would be the one person who had good reason to despise him and everything he represented. He knew Angel had rebuffed every offer Riverside had made for her property along the river. That hadn't surprised him in the least. He knew how much that land had meant to her father. But no one had bothered to inform him until today that she was also a member of the Crossfield town council, that she represented the contingent of Crossfield citizens who were adamantly opposed to change.

He let his gaze slide over her, greedily detailing each lovely feature—that glorious red hair, worn long now judging by the thick twist at her nape, and eyes that were still the most beguiling shade of green he'd ever seen. She'd grown so incredibly gorgeous, he thought, with a sharp tightening in his stomach. So womanly.

The past ten years had added a poise and self-confidence that were astonishing, a maturity that was breathtaking. She had always been beautiful to him, more beautiful by far than any woman he'd ever known. She and Aiden had been identical in appearance, yet he'd never once mistaken one for the other. Not once. That hadn't been an excuse he could use.

With a bitter tinge of regret, he tried to look away, but his gaze kept coming back to her. He had the sudden urge to spirit her away from here, to take her somewhere quiet and romantic where the lights were dim and he could slide his hand along the creamy expanse of her legs, so stunningly displayed beneath the hem of her short skirt. He longed to trace his finger along the neck of her silk tank top, exploring the soft fabric that only hinted at the enticement hidden underneath. But most of all, he wanted to remove, one by one, the pins that held in place that prim knot of hair and watch the fiery cascade tumble down her back in wanton abandonment. He wanted to kiss her long and hard until everything and everyone spun away from them.

With a healthy dose of reality, he tamped down that reckless urge. He was here to do a job, he reminded himself grimly. And that job required him to make peace with Angel Lowell, win her over, sell her on the prospect of the future. Better to keep their past out of it.

He saw her gaze shift, and for one brief moment found himself hopelessly sinking into those endless green depths. She quickly shuttered her eyes, closing him out, and he reluctantly turned his attention back to Mayor Sikes, who was exuberantly introducing him. Drew stood and took the podium.

He smiled warmly as he let his gaze roam the audience. "As I recall, the last time I was brought before a Crossfield town meeting had something to do with Halloween night and an outhouse placed on top of city hall. I must say, my task here tonight is a bit more pleasant than it was that night."

The tension in the room began to evaporate as everyone laughed their approval. Ann felt the corners of her own mouth twitch. She remembered how Drew and her cousin, Jack Hudson, had struggled to load Fannie Taylor's outhouse into the back of Jack's old pickup truck while she and

Aiden had kept lookout. How they'd managed to get it on top of city hall, she'd never dared ask.

Mayor Sikes had been livid, and he'd insisted Jack and Drew come before a town meeting and publicly apologize to Fannie and to the whole town. Now he was laughing more uproariously over that incident than anyone else, his belly shaking like the Pillsbury Doughboy in a pin-striped suit.

Drew let the laughter subside, his own grin fading as he surveyed the crowd once more, his gaze pausing briefly on Ann before sweeping on. But she'd felt a warming impact from even so fleeting a glance from those blue, blue eyes.

"As most of you know, Riverside Development is a division of Braeden Industries of Dallas, the firm I've been employed by since graduating from UT. My background in Crossfield gives me a unique appreciation of small town values and concerns. At the same time, my long-time standing with Braeden Industries and now with Riverside Development enables me to tell you without hesitation that they can bring much to this community."

Drew's commanding air of self-confidence had an immediate effect on the crowd. Except for the smooth, liquid tones of his voice, a dropped pin could have been heard in that room.

Ann bit her lip in consternation as she took in the absorbed faces around her. He had them in the palm of his hand already, she thought with a sinking heart. He was seducing every last one of them without batting an eye. Even Viola Pickles's austere features were tempered, and Bernice and Wilma looked positively enraptured.

"What Riverside is proposing, ladies and gentlemen, is a partnership. A partnership that will ensure a bright and prosperous future for generations of Crossfield citizens.

"I'll be around for a while, several weeks in fact, meeting with Mayor Sikes and the town council as well as various special interest groups and individuals." Again his eyes grazed Ann. "If you have any questions or concerns or comments, please feel free to come to me with them. Mayor Sikes?"

"Thank you, Drew. I'm sure everyone joins me in saying welcome home. Now, does anyone have any questions?"

Evidently, Mayor Sikes's re-emergence worked like a dousing of cold water on Wilma and Bernice. Both of them were on their feet, hands raised high.

With a glare of disapproval over his bifocals, Mayor Sikes said, "Bernice? You have a question?"

"I certainly do," she stated emphatically, directing her question to Drew. "Just what is your company's intentions concerning all those old houses along Riverside Drive? Young man, you can't come in here, bulldozing away the past without regard to the heritage of our town. Many of those houses have great historical value, not to mention the families who still live in them."

"Miss Ballard, Riverside Development is not forcing anyone out of their homes. We're making legitimate offers to property owners along the river, and frankly, many of them have responded quite favorably."

"And if that area is rezoned for commercial building, what will become of the ones who don't want to sell?" Wilma chimed in. "They'll end up with parking lots and convenience stores for next door neighbors."

"That will be a matter for the town council to decide. As you know, Riverside's request for rezoning the waterfront has not yet been accepted by the council."

"And never will be," Viola proclaimed loudly. "Right, Ann? Ann?"

Ann jumped slightly as Viola nudged her into awareness. She looked around at all the expectant faces waiting for her to take up their cause. A sense of overwhelming vulnerability washed over her. She knew what had to be done, what needed to be said, but all she seemed to be able to focus on was how utterly compelling Drew's eyes still were, how openly inviting his mouth had always been—

"I have serious reservations about these proposals," she said finally. Several women from the Historical Society turned in their chairs to stare at her, and Bernice, Wilma and Viola were openly gaping. "Very serious reservations," she added lamely.

"That's why I'm here," Drew said, looking directly at her with those vivid, penetrating eyes. "I want to hear all your concerns and questions. All I ask is that I be given a chance to present my side."

The warm, enveloping sound of his voice aroused tremors all through her, and Ann had to wonder whether they were still talking about the development project or something more personal—something much more threatening.

She forced a challenge into her gaze as she turned to face Drew. "And those of us who oppose this project want the same consideration. The farmers around here have had a lot of tough years. For those who want to sell Riverside their land, the escalating property values are wonderful. But to those of us who don't wish to sell, and never will, the increase in property taxes will be just another burden for us to carry." She paused for a moment, her chin lifting slightly as she continued to defy Drew. "You seem to think that your development plan will somehow give Crossfield a better way of life, but a lot of us think it's just fine the way it is. We don't call escalating crime rates, traffic jams and the destruction of the countryside 'a bright and prosperous future.'"

"Here! Here!" Bernice applauded, only to be targeted by Mayor Sikes's deepening scowl.

"I'm not denying there's a price to be paid for progress," Drew said calmly. "But the rewards are often greater. Crossfield has lived in the past too long. It's time to take a step forward before this town goes the way of so many other farming communities these days."

There were murmurs of assent from the crowd. Nathan Bennett, one of Ann's neighbors and an avid supporter of the development project, stood up, his face flushed dark red with excitement and possibly a nip or two of something else. "You're right, Drew. Some of us are more concerned with the opportunities your project could bring—like jobs and new businesses, better schools and roads. How do a few termite-infested old houses down by the river compare with our children's futures? We don't want the deal queered by a bunch of old battle-axes who don't have anything better to do with their time—"

Bernice was back on her feet in a flash. "Now, see here, Nat Bennett, I'll have you know I'm just as concerned with your children's welfare as you are. Maybe more so, judging by the condition that house of yours is in—"

Mayor Sikes's gavel sounded over the dull roar of the crowd. "Now, hold on a minute. We're all friends and neighbors here. No need to get so hot under the collar. We can state our opinions and concerns without getting personal. I think we've all said enough for tonight. More will be accomplished if we let Drew take up these matters one on one rather than in a shouting match. This meeting stands adjourned. Cake and coffee's been set up in the lobby—"

"Come on, girls," Bernice said, gathering up her purse and placard. "We need to plot a new strategy."

"Now, wait a minute," Viola protested, trailing after Bernice. "I'm the president. I think I should be the one to decide—"

"Wilma! Are you going to sit there all night or are you coming with us?"

Ann let the voices swirl around her as she stood. For just a moment her gaze caught Drew's and a spark of something—anger?—ignited between them. Then she turned, tucking her purse beneath her arm, and walked out of the room.

Two

Ann stood on her front porch, letting the night surround her like a soft, velvet cocoon. She'd been home from the meeting for over an hour, but had only gone inside long enough to dispense with her shoes and stockings. Out here, with the cool breeze from the river gliding along her bare arms and legs, the evening was like a fragrant balm.

Down by the river the crickets and bullfrogs had begun their evening serenade. The leaves rustled overhead, sounding like rain, and the scent of roses and honeysuckle carried on the wind as heady and maddening as a drug. Ann rested her head against a wooden support, blinking back a mist of unfamiliar tears at the memories the summer night whispered to her. Warm, starry evenings, the sliding shimmer of the river, and she and Drew swimming in the moonlight...

Somewhere in the distance a car engine sounded on the highway. Ann waited for it to bypass the turnoff to the farm, but it didn't. Instead she watched the headlights bouncing down the gravel road toward her. She watched as the beautiful, gleaming car came around the last bend in the lane and stopped at the end of the driveway. She watched as the driver got out of the car and came slowly across the yard toward her.

Only then did she realize she'd been holding her breath. She let it out with an almost painful swoosh.

Drew stopped at the steps, one foot poised on the bottom stair as he met her eyes in the moonlight. The pale, silvery light cast an ethereal glow between them, making the moment seem even more unreal, like a dream. Then a ghost of a smile touched his lips, and Ann's heart slowly contracted.

"What are you doing here?" she asked. There was a strange catch to her voice that disturbed her. She tried to swallow it away as she continued to hold Drew's gaze.

"I didn't get a chance to talk to you at the meeting. I wanted to come out here and explain my situation to you."

"There's no need. You made it perfectly clear," Ann said, forcing a calmness into her tone she was far from feeling. "And I'll try to make mine just as clear. If you've come out here to make me an offer, you're wasting your time."

His smile twisted wryly. "So I've heard." He paused briefly, climbing up another step or two so that eyes were on an even level. Ann moved back a step. Drew stopped. For a moment he stood there looking at her, his heart pounding at her nearness. She leaned her back against the porch post as she faced him defiantly, but with her bare feet and legs, her hair wisping about her face, she looked touchingly vulnerable and young, so incredibly sweet—and to him, at least, so very unreachable.

Keep it light, he advised himself sternly. She was like a wild, skittish colt. One false move on his part, and she would be gone, lost. "That was quite a cheering section you had back there. I hadn't realized until tonight you were leading the opposition."

"I'm not," she denied. "I mean, I'm not a member of the Historical Society or any other group. But as a council member, I have to listen to the needs and desires of all the citizens, and there are a lot of people around here who don't want this project going through."

"But a lot of people do," he insisted. "And as a council member, you have to be willing to listen to both sides, right?"

"Who says I'm not?" she challenged, lifting her chin a notch. "Riverside's done a lot of talking in the past few months, and I haven't liked much of what I've heard. What you're proposing will change the whole complexion of the town, turn it into some sort of riverside resort with a bunch of overpriced homes sitting on so many undersized lots. Crossfield is a small town, Drew. Personally, I'd like to see it stay that way."

"Everybody's entitled to his or her opinion," Drew said without rancor. "All I ask is that I be given a chance to try and change it."

Ann bristled indignantly. "I doubt you can do that."

He smiled, his voice intimately low and persuasive. "All I ask is a fair chance." He emphasized the word fair.

"Is that why you came all the way out here tonight?" Ann asked coolly. "To make sure I wouldn't sabotage your project on personal bias?"

Drew shrugged. "Partly. And partly because I wanted to see you, talk to you, maybe make it a little easier on both of us when we meet up from now on. And we will be meeting, often. Circumstances have thrown us together, and everyone's going to be watching us, pouncing on any animosity between us to feed their curiosity."

"Are you saying you're worried about gossip?" Ann asked incredulously. "As I recall, you never cared one way or the other what people said or thought."

"That's not altogether true," he objected, his words falling like rose petals on the sultry night air. "I always valued your opinion, Angel."

No one but Drew had ever been able to make her childish name sound so seductive. The intimacy of it now tore at Ann's heart. The years faded away and he was once again Drew, her first love, the boy next door who could wrap her around his little finger with just a smile or a touch or the whisper of her name. Regret spilled through her, but it was only a dim reflection of the pain and bitterness and disillusionment she had once suffered because of this man.

She let her eyes meet Drew's once more as she folded her arms in front of her, forcing herself to remain calm and undaunted beneath the power of his devastating blue gaze. "No one calls me Angel anymore. At least not to my face."

"Sorry. Old habits, as they say, die hard." He mounted the rest of the steps, coming to stand beside her so that she was forced to look up at him. "I'd heard you'd changed your name sometime ago."

From Aiden, of course, Ann thought with a prick of an emotion she did not care to identify.

"In fact, it's now Dr. Lowell, I believe."

She heard the light, almost teasing quality in his voice and found herself responding in spite of her resolve. A grudging smile touched her lips. "Since you're not one of my students, Ann will do." She paused, then added, almost accusingly, "We've certainly heard great things about your career. Vice president, isn't it?"

Drew gave a low, ironic laugh. "One of several. Empty titles to feed our egos rather than our bank balances."

His self-deprecating humor somehow managed to cut through the tension. Ann felt her taut muscles slowly begin to relax as she allowed herself to respond to Drew's smile.

A furtive movement in the garden below captured their attention. Ann could just make out the dark outline of her three-legged cat as he crouched at the edge of a flowerbed, eyes glowing in the darkness. He pounced at some poor, unfortunate creature in the grass, one gray paw whipping out like a hook. With a loud meow of protest, he disappeared into the foliage, stalking.

"One of your infamous strays, no doubt," Drew teased warmly.

Ann nodded. "I found him out on the highway a few months ago where he had been hit by a car and left to die. Dr. Matlock patched him up as best he could, but there wasn't anything he could do about his leg. He manages just fine with the three he has left, though," she remarked proudly. "Watson's very curious, always prowling around, poking in corners. And he's smart as a whip."

"Then why not Sherlock?" Drew asked with an easy laugh. "You always did find heroes in the most unlikely guises."

The sound of his laughter touched something deep inside her, something she tried to deny but couldn't. His laughter still had the power to set her stomach quivering, her hands to trembling. It still had the power to break through all the barriers she had so carefully erected. "Not anymore," she said in a tone that held the faintest trace of resentment. "I gave up looking for heroes a long time ago."

The momentary break in tension fled at her words. She noted the slight stiffening of his posture that acknowledged the same thought.

"Ang—Ann, I was sorry to hear about your father. And Aiden." He paused for a moment. "I wanted to talk to you at her service, but there were a lot of people around you...I didn't want to intrude."

Her soft green eyes impaled him with a piercing glance. "I was surprised to hear you were there at all."

He shrugged uneasily, his voice slightly defensive. "A lot of people were, I imagine. It seemed to me the decent thing to do."

"Yes. As I recall, you were always big on doing the decent thing—at least where Aiden was concerned."

Ann felt a small prickle of remorse as she watched a brief frown crease Drew's forehead at her bitter words. Her response had been automatic, prompted by emotions in herself that were all too easy to identify. When someone had first told her that Drew had been at the service, Ann's heart had almost hit the floor. For a brief terrible moment, even in her grief, she'd felt the threat of an old jealousy. Then there had been the inevitable and almost instantaneous feeling of guilt. Those same two emotions had warred inside her for ten long years.

"Look, I'm sorry," she said abruptly. "That was uncalled for."

"You've every right," Drew acknowledged. But something flashed in those blue depths, something dark and unfathomable, leaving Ann wondering about the hardened look in his eyes.

Her earlier impression of him had been wrong, she realized suddenly. He *had* changed. A great deal. Even in the moonlight, she could see the lines around his mouth and eyes were far more deeply etched than she had first judged. It would have been a kindness to call them laugh lines when Ann somehow knew they weren't. They gave him a visage far more mature than his thirty years.

"That was all a long time ago," she said softly, reminding herself as well as him. It had been a long time ago. The years had slipped away and taken their youth. They had each lived their lives and time hadn't stopped for either of them. "Why are you really here, Drew? What do you want from me?"

His eyes raked her face, then looked away. She wondered suddenly and unpleasantly in the silence that followed whether he'd found the changes in her own face as disturbing as she'd found those in his.

What did he expect? she thought bitterly. Ten years wrought changes in everyone. So did pain and disillusionment and anger.

"I want your goodwill, Ann," he said at last. "No matter what the outcome of the Riverside project turns out to be. This may sound strange to you, but I'd like to establish some sort of—I don't know—peace between us. I want to put the past to rest once and for all."

Ann plucked a chandelier of honeysuckle from the trellis beside her and spun the blossom beneath her nose like a tiny pinwheel. She closed her eyes as the thick, haunting scent triggered a thousand memories. Abruptly her eyes opened. "You're a little late to be asking for my goodwill."

He fixed her with a long, searching gaze. "It's been ten years, Ann. I can't believe you still hate me that much."

"You flatter yourself. Hate is a powerful emotion. I don't feel anything for you anymore."

"Is that why you ran away from me earlier? You ran away from me a long time ago, and you're doing it still. What are you afraid of?"

She gaped at him in open-mouthed indignation. "I'm certainly not afraid of you!" she snapped in sudden anger.

"Then why did you leave like that?" he asked softly. "Why did you leave without telling me where you were going, without even saying goodbye?"

For a moment she thought he was still talking about her leaving the meeting, but when she realized he was referring to the past, her gaze sliced him with scorn. "I can't believe you're asking me that. You, of all people, know exactly why I left, why I had to."

"You didn't have to," Drew argued reasonably, as though the discussion was no more important than idle dinner conversation. "You could have stayed and given me a chance to work something out."

Her laughter had a bitter, hollow ring to it that had them both blanching. "You got married, remember? You had a child on the way. What could we possibly have 'worked out'?"

"I never meant to hurt you."

She merely stared at him, crushing the honeysuckle blossom tightly in her fist. Abruptly turning away from him, she threw it, lifeless, to the ground.

"It was only one night." Drew's voice had grown quietly insistent, as though he meant to have his say whether she wanted to hear him or not. "I made a terrible mistake, but you would never let me explain. You wouldn't even try to understand."

Ann whirled around, her cheeks burning with indignation, her eyes glittering like green embers. "What was there to understand, for God's sake? You betrayed me!"

"And you sure as hell didn't take long to get over it, did you?" Drew blazed, his temper quick and explosive, as though anger had been simmering all along, just beneath the surface.

Ann stared at him in speechless outrage. That he could presume to know what she had endured! The pain, the loneliness, the sheer hell. She rallied her anger, not bothering to confirm or deny his allegation.

"How dare you say that to me?" Her voice shook with the unleashed emotion of a decade as she clenched her hands into white fists of fury.

"Truth hurts, does it?" Drew taunted cruelly. "I've had to face ten long damned years of truth, Angel. You ran away without a word and it took you, what?—all of six months to find a replacement—"

In the strained silence that fell between them the slap resounded like a tree that had been split by lightning. Ann saw the glaring red on the left side of Drew's face, saw the blue of his eyes darken to a deep and dangerous indigo. She took a faltering step backward.

"Get out of here!" The words were more forceful this time, but she had to turn away, had to put a hand to her lips to quell the trembling.

She felt rather than saw Drew stride angrily down the steps and across the yard. She looked up to see him at his car, his hand poised over the handle. He was looking back at her, but the darkness cloaked his expression.

"Just tell me one thing," he demanded coldly. "Why is it you could forgive Aiden, but you could never forgive me?"

At the sound of his car door slamming, Ann collapsed weakly onto the porch swing, telling herself it was all over now. She could relax. She was safe here in her little world. She could hear the crickets chirping, could feel the soft, night air against her flushed face as it stirred the wayward tendrils of hair at her nape and temples. Everything was as it should be. She could forget Drew Maitland.

But almost like a warning, his car engine leaped to life, intruding into her private domain. He gunned the motor unnecessarily as he turned the powerful car, and with a sputter of gravel, roared down the narrow lane at a furious clip. His brake lights flashed momentarily as he approached the highway, and then he was gone into the night.

Ann tried to muster up the relief she knew she should be feeling but she was too numb, too dazed. Her eyes fluttered closed for a moment.

Her first instinct on seeing him walk across the yard toward her, even after everything that had happened between them, had been to run down the steps and throw herself into his arms, to cling to the protective shelter she'd once found there.

And what a horribly embarrassing mistake that would have been. The man she'd once loved was gone from her forever. He'd made his choice a long time ago, and she'd had to learn to live with it. At least she thought she had until the moment their eyes had first met after the long years between them...

"Oh, God," she whispered raggedly, opening her eyes, seeing the comforting surroundings of her porch waver into focus. With trembling hands, she pushed back a tangled wisp of red hair from her forehead.

Why hadn't she been enough? How many times in the past ten years had she asked herself that question? How many times had she provided herself with the same brutal answer?

Because Aiden had been more. Aiden, her twin sister who had had the same looks as Ann, but with the personality and confidence to use them. Aiden, who had never been afraid to go after what she wanted, and she'd wanted Drew.

Drew had wanted Aiden, too, Ann reminded herself relentlessly. He'd wanted her enough to make love to her. He'd wanted her enough to marry her, to stay married to her even after Aiden had lost the baby. For three long years, he'd stayed with her. And then Aiden had wanted out.

For the next seven years, with both he and Ann free and clear, Drew hadn't so much as called her. In many ways that was the deepest hurt of all, the hardest to forgive. For years she'd kept her life on hold, wishing and waiting for Drew Maitland to come back to her.

Those long, empty years were like dust in her throat now.

Ann held her hands out in front of her. They were still trembling. She squeezed them together, trying to stop the shaking, trying to block the torrent of memories flooding over her, drowning her, pulling her back to a place she did not want to go....

"Happy birthday, Angel."

"Oh, Drew, look! A shooting star. Do you suppose that was meant just for me, so I can have another wish?" Perched on the top rail of the fence, her face lifted to the star-studded sky, Angel felt the slow drift of the river breeze skimming across her skin. Drew stood on the ground facing her, his arms wrapped securely about her waist.

She felt the smooth caress of his hand along her back as he smiled up at her. "Of course. Angels take care of their own, don't they?"

She bent down suddenly, touching her lips to his. He responded immediately, tightening his arms around her, deepening the kiss with his tongue. Angel let herself enjoy the sensations rippling through her body for a moment longer before she pulled back. Drew sighed heavily as he lay his head against her chest. Her fingers trailed softly through the thick strands of his hair.

"I missed you so." He breathed the words against her neck as his lips found her rapidly beating pulse. "I was miserable without you."

She smiled as she kissed his hair. "You can't live with me and you can't live without me."

"Only half that's true."

"Which half?" Angel teased lightly.

"You know damn well which half," Drew growled roughly. His arms tightened around her, then lifted her off the fence. He hauled her against the hardness of his body, holding her captive in his arms while his mouth claimed hers once more. His tongue parted her lips, then dipped inside, exploring almost desperately the deep recesses of her mouth. Angel moaned softly, feeling the need of her body to respond, yet still holding back.

"Drew, please," she whispered softly as his mouth left hers to trail along her neck, his tongue skimming across her skin.

"Angel, I want you so much. I need you." His voice was an urgent whisper against her ear. "We can't go on like this."

Angel swallowed past the rise of panic in her throat. "Do you think we should break up again?"

"No. Breaking up was your idea, remember? I think we should get married."

She stared up at him in shock. "But... we still have the same problems, Drew. You want to live in the city, and I don't. I can't leave the farm, and I can't leave Dad. He needs me. You know how he relies on me."

"Yes, I know," Drew said, almost bitterly. "But don't worry. I won't ever ask you to choose between your family and me again. If moving to the city means giving you up, then it's not worth it. We'll stay. I'll find a job here after I graduate. But I don't want to wait to get married, Angel. I don't think we should."

Angel felt a vague sense of unease at the urgency in his tone, but her elation soon swept it away. Wasn't this what she'd always wanted ever since she'd first set eyes on Drew Maitland?

She smiled through a mist of tears. "I don't think we should wait, either. Oh, Drew, you won't be sorry. I'll make you so happy! We can be together at last... in every way," she added shyly.

Drew's blue eyes blazed with an inner fire. "Are you sure about this? I don't want to pressure you, Angel."

She laughed lightly, tilting her head to gaze up at him. "You aren't pressuring me. I've wanted this forever."

He laughed, too, lifting her off the ground and spinning her around in the moonlight. He brought her back down to earth, then pulled a box from his pocket and handed it to her. "In that case, you'd better open your birthday present."

"Oh, Drew." Ann's hands shook slightly as she took the blue velvet box from his hand and opened it. The diamond that twinkled inside was as bright and beautiful as the stars overhead. "It's beautiful!" she breathed.

"It's not very big," Drew apologized as he lifted the ring from the soft bed and slipped it on her finger. "Someday I'll replace it with a larger one."

"You'll do no such thing," Angel cried, appalled at the notion. "I'll never take this ring off. Do you hear me? Never!"

The house was quiet when Angel tiptoed in sometime after midnight. She climbed the stairs, knowing exactly which step to avoid to prevent a telltale creak. She slipped down the hallway, past her father's darkened room, until she reached her own at the end. She paused. A thin sliver of light shone beneath Aiden's door across the hall. Angel held up her hand to the moonlight flowing in from the hall window. The diamond winked at her.

She had to tell someone. She knew she would burst with the news if she had to wait until morning. She knocked softly on Aiden's door. "Aiden?" She cracked the door. "Are you awake?"

"No."

Her sister's voice sounded suspiciously muffled, as though she'd been crying. Angel pushed open the door and walked into the room. Her sister was lying on her side, her knees drawn up to her chest. A wet washcloth was draped across her forehead.

"Are you sick?" Angel asked worriedly. "What's wrong?"

"I don't know. I just don't feel well," Aiden mumbled, rolling onto her back. "What do you want, anyway?"

In spite of her sister's illness, Angel couldn't help smiling. She sat down on the edge of the bed and held out her hand. "Aiden, I have the most incredible news. Look! Drew and I are engaged."

Aiden's head turned slowly toward her, her gaze dropping to Angel's extended hand. Aiden's face crumpled suddenly, and she turned her head away, covering her face with the washcloth.

"Aiden, what's wrong? What is it?" But her sister's sobs only grew louder. Feeling the first sliver of panic, Angel got up and closed the bedroom door. She came back to stand over the bed. "Aiden, you'd better tell me what's wrong."

A pause, then, "I'm pregnant."

At first Angel thought she must have heard her wrong, but the words slowly sank in, and she felt her breath leave her body in a painful rush. Knees shaking, she sat down heavily on the bed.

"Are you sure?"

"I haven't been to the doctor, but, yes, I'm sure." Aiden's sobs had subsided, but her voice still held a hint of hysteria.

"Who—?"

For the first time since Angel had entered her room, Aiden met her gaze. Angel felt a hard knot of apprehension twisting in her stomach.

"Drew."

Angel's heart contracted with the force and pain of a physical blow. Fear, as sharp and piercing as a knife, sliced through her veins. Stunned, she stared at Aiden, striving for breath. "You're lying!" she finally gasped. "Why would you say such a thing? How could you be so cruel, Aiden?"

"I'm not lying," Aiden denied angrily.

"How could you do this to me?" Angel screamed, jumping up from the bed and whirling toward the door. She couldn't stand to look at Aiden's face, couldn't bear to think that there could be even a remote chance her sister was telling the truth.

"You broke up with him two months ago. You said it was over," Aiden said, her voice suddenly sounding calm. "I didn't think you'd get back together. It just happened."

Angel wanted to slap her sister, slap that tear-stained face until she made Aiden admit she was lying. But what if she wasn't?

"I don't believe you," she whispered desperately, as much for her own benefit as Aiden's. "And I'll never forgive you for this, Aiden!" Angel spun around and fled the room, her heart hammering painfully against her chest. Weak-kneed, her head spinning, she supported herself against the wall outside Aiden's door. She closed her eyes against the fear, the dread.

Moments later she climbed over the fence separating the Lowell and Maitland property, and stood looking up at Drew's open window. His light was still on, and she watched for long, heartsick moments as he paced back and forth across his room.

"Drew." She called his name softly, aware that his parent's bedroom was on the other side of the house. "Drew!"

He came to the window and looked out. "Angel? What are you doing?"

"I need to talk to you."

Something in her voice must have alerted him. He stood silently for a moment, gazing down at her. "I'll be right down."

"Is it true?" she demanded when they stood face to face at the edge of the yard.

"Angel, what are you talking about?" he asked guardedly.

Already she could read the truth in his eyes. "You and Aiden. Is it true?" she repeated. She turned away from his stricken expression. "Never mind. You just answered my question." She pulled the ring from her finger and hurled it toward his chest. For just an instant it was a flashing arc in the moonlight, a falling star, before it dropped to the ground and died.

Drew grabbed her arm as she tried to run away. "Angel, wait. Please, let me explain. It's not what you think. It was only one night—"

"It only takes one night to make a baby, Drew."

Even in the moonlight, she could see the color drain from his face. "Oh, God, no—"

"Oh, God, yes," she mocked cruelly. "And just what are you going to do about it?" She jerked her arm from his grasp and left him, stunned, while she turned and ran back along the path toward home.

The lights were blazing in the house when she got there. Aiden had already spread the news, Angel guessed angrily. She let herself into the house and stood at the open door of her father's study for a moment. Adam Lowell, his gray head resting wearily against the back of his leather chair, looked as though he'd aged ten years. A glass of Scotch sat untouched on the desk in front of him. Some small movement of Angel's must have caught his attention, for he looked up. Immediately he stood and opened his arms to her. She fled into them.

He held her for several moments while, for the first time since her mother had died years ago, she wept openly in his arms. He held her and soothed her hair, and then he pushed her gently away.

"The time for tears is over now, Angel. You've had your cry. Now it's time to look ahead. Your sister needs you."

Angel pulled away in protest. "How can you say that? After what she did to me!"

"What's done is done," Adam replied calmly. "I never thought you and Drew were a match anyway. I always expected him to break your heart. Aiden needs him now. Don't stand in their way, Angel."

She couldn't believe what she was hearing. She and Drew had belonged together ever since they'd met four years ago. She'd only been fourteen and he sixteen, but even then they'd known what they had was special. How could her father even suggest that *she* was standing in the way. It was Aiden. Always Aiden.

Adam's position, however, remained firm. Calmly, gently but resolutely, he pointed out how difficult a time Aiden would have if she were to have the baby alone. In a town as small as Crossfield, an illegitimate baby was still very much a stigma. There would be gossip; Aiden's life would be ruined.

What about my life? Angel wanted to scream. What about me? But she already knew what her father's answer would be. Angel was the sensible one, the smart one. Angel was always the dutiful daughter and sister. She knew what had to be done, the *right* thing to be done. In time, she'd get over this. In time, she'd meet someone else....

Angel flew from her father's study and up the stairs to her own room, slamming the door behind her. She was vaguely aware that the phone started ringing and barely registered when someone picked up, only to have it ring again a minute or two later. She huddled beneath the covers of her bed, feeling devastated, betrayed, and utterly alone.

"Angel? Angel, answer me."

She could hear Aiden calling to her from the hallway as her sister jiggled the knob on the locked door. "Angel, please let me come in."

"Leave me alone, Aiden."

"I'm sorry, Angel. I'm sorry you're hurt. It happened—"

"Shut up!" Angel barely realized she was screaming the words. "Shut up, Aiden! I don't want to hear how it happened! I never want to talk to you again, do you hear me? I hate you! I hate you! I wish you were dead!"

Angel pulled the covers over her head, blocking the outside world, shutting out the pounding in her head, the pounding on the front door. Even when she heard Drew downstairs, urgently shouting up to her, she shut him out, as well.

Angel left town the next day. Her father arranged for her to visit a friend in Los Angeles for a while. After a few weeks she decided to enroll in UCLA, eventually completing her graduate studies there and securing a professorship in the history department. For eight long years she'd stayed away, until her father had called her home before he'd died. Even then, his last thoughts had been of Aiden.

"I'm leaving the farm to you, Angel. Aiden would sell the land, squander the money, but I know I can count on you to hang onto it. This place is all your mother and I ever had, all we ever worked for. I promised her before she died the land would be our legacy to you and Aiden. I'm depending on you to see that it stays in the family. With Jack managing her trust fund and you the land, I'll rest easier knowing Aiden will always be taken care of.

"I know there's still a rift between you two. Don't bother denying it, I can see it in your eyes every time her name's mentioned. But she's your sister, Angel. There's no bond stronger than that. I want you to forgive her, as much for your sake as for hers."

Seeing him lying there, so pale and weak and clinging to her hand, Ann hadn't the heart to deny him anything.

So she came back home as her father expected her to, and in doing so, she realized that all the changes she had forced upon herself since leaving had only been superficial. She was still Angel Lowell, and changing her name had changed little else.

But at least one part of the promise had been kept. She had held onto the land. Forgiving Aiden hadn't been so easy.

She'd tried. God, she'd tried, but Ann could never feel the same about her sister. Even when Aiden had started reaching out to her again, Ann had never been able to think about her without feeling resentment and anger, and she could never forget that Drew had chosen Aiden over her.

"You're wrong, Drew," Ann whispered brokenly into the silence of the night. She'd never forgiven Aiden, and now it was too late. What was more, the message Aiden had sent her the night she'd died proved that, even in death, Aiden had still been reaching out to her, and Ann had not been able to help her.

I wish you were dead. How that one hateful sentence had haunted her all these months since her twin's fatal accident. The jealousy that had festered inside her for so many years had then turned to guilt, an emotion just as destructive and just as binding.

And now Drew was back, reminding her so painfully why she and Aiden had gotten lost from each other in the first place. He'd taken almost everything from her once, and now he'd come back to try and take her home, to try and make her break a vow that had been all she'd had to give to her father.

Impatiently, Ann wiped the back of her hand across the dampness on her cheeks. She could almost hear her father admonishing her—over a scraped knee, a bad grade, a broken heart— "Here now, no more tears. Since when do Angels cry?"

Since she'd met Drew Maitland all those years ago.

Three

Drew clattered down the metal steps outside his room at the Crossfield Motel, then checked his stride as he spotted the figure reclining against the front fender of his Jaguar.

Dressed in faded jeans, a white T-shirt and a used-up pair of tennis shoes, this man was yet another image from Drew's past. And the look of wary distrust he wore was only slightly more welcoming than Ann's had been last night.

"'Morning," the man remarked in a voice that sounded neither cool nor friendly, but not totally indifferent, either. "Nice car. Yours, I presume?"

Drew smiled slightly. "You don't think I'd come driving into Crossfield, Texas, in a stolen car, do you?"

One dark brow shot up. "Wouldn't be the first time you took a car out joyriding, now would it?"

"If you're referring to the incident with the Mercedes, I believe that was your idea."

"You were driving," came the lazy response.

"And as I recall, that didn't make one iota of difference to your mother. Maddie took a frying pan to both our butts."

They grinned simultaneously at the memory, the awkwardness between them fading. "Imagine that," Jack Hudson said ruefully, shaking his head. "Sixteen years old and my mother spanking me in front of my best friend."

Drew chuckled. "The best friend got it just as hard as you did. I couldn't sit down for a week, but I must say, I lost my affinity for Dad's new Mercedes in a hurry. Your mother could be very persuasive."

"Couldn't she?" Jack agreed ruefully.

"What are you doing up and around this time of the morning?" Drew asked with a certain amount of suspicion.

"You forget I was raised on a farm. Half the day's gone. Besides, I knew you had a meeting with Sam McCauley this morning. I wanted to catch you before you left."

Drew stared at him for a moment, his eyes narrowing. "How the hell did you know that?"

Jack grinned crookedly, and for the first time his expression took on a hint of the devil-may-care look he'd always sported as a teenager.

Back in the old days Jack Hudson had been the most carefree soul Drew had ever met. They'd been kindred spirits from the moment their paths crossed. If Drew's parents had thought moving and getting their growing boy out of the city would keep him out of trouble, they hadn't figured on Jack Hudson and his twin cousins. They had been holy terrors that first summer, and Drew had quickly become their willing accomplice. They might all have ended up in reform school or worse if Angel hadn't kept a sensible head for all of them. Their guardian Angel, they'd teased her. She hadn't much appreciated that, Drew remembered wryly.

"Haven't you learned yet that every move you make in this town is reported five minutes later by no fewer than a dozen eye witnesses? Nothing's secret in Crossfield. You should know that as well as anybody."

"Yeah, well, I guess some things never change," Drew said dryly.

"Some don't," Jack agreed, his expression sobering as his gaze cut back to Drew. "But Ann has."

"What's that supposed to mean?"

"I hear you drove out to see her last night after the meeting."

Drew shrugged. "So? I'm seeing and talking to a lot of people. Ann's a member of the town council as well as a property owner. Why wouldn't I go see her? I'm sure you've heard that's why I'm here," he added with a faint trace of bitterness.

"As long as that's all it is." Jack's voice was low and even, but there was a subtle note of warning in it. He stared thoughtfully at the toes of his worn Nikes for a moment. "Frankly, as Ann's attorney, I've advised her all along to sell to Riverside. She's spent a mint on that old house the last couple of years—a new roof last year, a new pump a couple of months ago. The plumbing's a constant battle, and the wiring—that's a nightmare in itself. Uncle Adam named me executor of his estate so that I could keep an eye on the trust funds he set up from their mother's inheritance, but Ann's is dwindling faster than I can keep up with it. I don't mind telling you, it worries me."

He paused for a moment, and Drew said, "I sense there's a 'but' in there somewhere."

Jack's gray eyes narrowed to a squint. "I don't want to see her hurt again."

"I have no intention of hurting Angel."

"I'm glad to hear it, because she's been through enough in the last several years. She's lost her father, she's lost her sister. Mom was like a mother to her and now she's moved to Houston. I'm all the family Ann has left around here, and I intend to look out for her. I wouldn't like to think that this sudden interest in her after all these years has anything to do with your company wanting to acquire her property."

Drew's head snapped around in a sudden blaze of anger. "I ought to punch your face in for that remark."

"Yeah, you probably should," Jack agreed amiably. "But I had to say it just the same." He ran an admiring hand over the dark green surface of the car hood. "Anyway, looks like you're doing all right for yourself."

Drew smiled coolly. "I could say the same about you," he said, nodding briefly in the direction of the new red Vette sitting beside the Jaguar.

"Yeah, I guess you could," Jack agreed. "But as we both know, appearances can be deceiving, can't they?"

It was still early, but the sun was already hot against her neck as Ann walked along the mossy bluff overlooking the river. Below her the wide green river slid along lofty banks where water irises grew in violet profusion in a morning light that was misty yellow. A white crane skimmed the glassy surface of the water, searching.

Rising over the treetops, she could see the rusted, towering rafters of the the old river bridge, which had been a ruin for as long as Ann could remember.

The very sight of that bridge always terrified her. Many of the iron supports were missing and the wooden floorboards had been rotting away for half a century. As children, she and Aiden and Jack had been instructed never to play there, but to Aiden and Jack, that had been the equivalent of putting ice cream before them and telling them not to eat it. The temptation became irresistible.

Ann could still remember standing on the road in the hot sun watching them walk across that bridge one summer afternoon. Her heart had pounded with fear, and her stomach had revolted from the terror. She'd lost her lunch right there in front of them, and Aiden and Jack had taunted her from the other side of the bridge, laughing at her and daring her to join them.

For a long time afterward, Ann had had recurring nightmares about that bridge, about seeing Aiden in the middle of it, one minute laughing and calling out to her, and the next minute gone. Ann would inevitably wake up screaming until she heard her father's brisk voice penetrating the nightmare and, reassured, would stop.

With a start Ann realized someone was on the bridge now, staring down at her from his lofty view. She shaded her eyes with her hand, and as she watched, he lifted a hand to wave at her.

"Drew?" She whispered the name in the early morning silence. What was *he* doing here? And on that bridge of all places! Didn't he know what that would do to her? Her stomach knotted painfully as she saw him start across the crumbling floorboards.

Her heart in her throat, she watched him near the end. Something buzzed past her cheek. Absently, she swatted the air, and then her movements froze as something struck the tree beside her with a loud *thwack.* A fraction of a second later the sharp crack of a rifle split the silence of the river.

For one heart-stopping moment she stood in stunned disbelief, her eyes still glued to Drew. Then terror sliced through her like a saber as reality sank in. Someone had been shooting in her direction, had almost hit her! Dazedly, she realized Drew was shouting something, a heated warning at the careless hunter, but she couldn't hear his exact words.

Behind her several thrushes were startled from a hedgerow. Ann whirled in panic at the sound, her toe snagging an exposed root. With a shriek she went sprawling to the ground, hands splayed wildly in front of her.

Panic detonated inside her at the sudden stillness all around her. Whether the hunter was moving toward her or away from her, she couldn't be sure. She lay motionless for several minutes, listening to the quiet.

"Ann! Where are you? Are you all right?"

Her head snapped to attention at the sound of Drew's voice. She looked around to find him sprinting through a clump of trees toward her. She tried to lift herself up, but her left wrist had twisted when she'd broken her fall. It refused to hold her weight now, and with a grunt of pain, she collapsed back onto the ground.

Drew was on his knees beside her in a flash. "Angel, are you all right? Are you hurt?"

"No, I'm okay. I tripped over something—"

His eyes closed briefly as he let out a quick breath. "Thank God. I heard the shot and then I heard you scream. When I saw you fall, I thought—"

"What are you doing here?" she asked as she struggled to get up again. Drew's hand shot out, grasping her arm as he helped her sit up.

"I had a breakfast meeting with Sam McCauley, and I decided to take a walk along the river afterward."

"And you decided to walk across that bridge?" she said with a note of censure in her tone.

"It's in worse shape than I remembered," he agreed wryly. "Listen, are you sure you're okay? What's the matter with your arm?"

"I twisted my wrist when I fell. It's nothing," Ann said shakily, trying to pull away. But Drew held her, gently but firmly, refusing to let her go.

"Let me take a look." His fingers tentatively explored along her wrist, probing the bones with a light, sure touch, reassuring them both that nothing was broken.

But Ann felt anything but reassured. His seeking fingers were touching more than just her skin. He was touching memories deep within her soul, awakening feelings she'd long ago buried. With each tender stroke, she could feel herself slipping away, drowning beneath a pool of emotion that should have been drained long, long ago. A soft sigh slipped through her lips, drawing his gaze to hers.

"Did I hurt you?" he asked in a strangely guarded tone.

More than you could ever imagine, she thought, but she only shook her head slightly, feeling the excitement of his touch spreading through her like a wildfire out of control.

He felt it, too. She could tell by the glint of wonder in his eyes, by the trace of some indefinable emotion in his features. His mouth had grown softer, luring her gaze. There had always been something so timelessly seductive about Drew's mouth. An image came to her now—she was standing beneath a full moon, wrapped in his arms, experiencing for the first time the wonder of his masculine lips against hers—

Mirroring her thoughts perfectly, Drew slowly lowered his head toward hers, the movement hypnotic as Ann stared up at him. Her lips parted slightly, waiting for that exquisitely torturous moment when his mouth would touch hers. Her eyes drifted closed. Her breath caught in her throat.

Yes. Oh, yes! This was the memory that had kept her awake at night, reliving in her mind his every touch, his every whisper, and then longing for more, so much more. This was the memory that had kept her alone and lonely for most of those ten years, because no man had ever been able to touch her as Drew had.

A storm of emotions ripped through her in that waiting moment, tearing her apart with the intensity, the longing.

Drew. He'd finally come back, and it was almost too easy to forget why. It was almost too easy not to care why, only that he was here, with her at last. She'd wanted this moment for so long, had wished for it desperately—

Be careful what you wish for, a little voice in the back of her mind taunted her. She'd had other wishes over the years, wishes that *had* come true and had tormented her ever since. She'd given up wishing a long time ago, especially where Drew Maitland was concerned.

Her hands fluttered weakly to his chest as she tried to gather her resistance, but still she couldn't find the strength to push him away.

Another shot rang out, farther down river. The hunter had obviously moved on, the danger was past, the enchantment shattered. Drew's head lifted as his hands fell away from her. They both struggled to their feet, then stepped apart as he whirled in the direction the shot had come from. "What the hell is going on here, a war?"

He turned back to her, looking as shaken as she felt, but that moment had given Ann the time to wipe away the tear she'd found coursing down her cheek. With an effort she fastened her mental armor back into place.

"Not yet," she tried to say lightly, but her voice trembled in spite of her best effort. "Just a few crazy, trigger-happy hunters."

"What the devil are they doing this close to the house?" he asked with a frown.

"That doesn't seem to bother these guys in the least," she said, forcing her gaze back to the woods as she waved a careless hand in that direction. "I've been having trouble for a couple of months now with poachers hunting on my land."

His scowl deepened. "I don't like the sound of that. Those shots were too damned close. Have you talked to Sheriff Hayden about this?"

"I've called him a few times, and he in turn has called the county game warden. But by the time either of them can get out here, the hunters are always long gone. Jack suggested I post the perimeters of my property with No Trespassing signs, and that seemed to help for a while. I guess they've decided to come back and take their chances."

"You're sure that's all it is?"

Ann looked at him in surprise. "What do you mean?"

Drew shrugged, his gaze uneasy as he surveyed the surrounding woods. "Mayor Sikes said there'd been a couple of incidents after the last council vote—a rock thrown through someone's window, some near fights in town."

"You think someone tried to shoot me because I'm opposing the development project?" Ann asked, seizing on the one topic she knew would buffer her from Drew's dangerous effect on her. "Seems to me you'd be the most likely suspect in that case."

His eyes met hers, issuing a challenge of his own. "I prefer to do my convincing in other ways." His blue gaze drifted over her and then came back up to once again meet her eyes. But he'd let her know with that one brief look that what had passed between them moments ago was not something he was going to forget. Or let *her* forget.

"I wasn't suggesting that someone deliberately tried to shoot you," he continued, his voice steady. "Whoever it was might have been trying to intimidate you, though, and got closer than he meant to. Nate Bennett's property adjoins yours, doesn't it?"

Ann nodded briefly. "Nate's a hothead, but he wouldn't do anything that foolhardy. More likely it's someone who's moved to the area recently to work in one of the new plants along the interstate. But that's part of the progress you seem to value so highly, isn't it? Strangers invading your privacy, escalating crime, noise pollution—just to mention a few."

Drew's posture remained casual, but anger flashed like summer lightning in his eyes at her derisive tone. "I suppose you'd rather sit back in your little retreat out here, and pretend the rest of the world doesn't exist. Crossfield was changing long before I ever got involved with Riverside Development. All those factories, the new airport not twenty miles away—it's all part of the surging growth in this area. You can't blame me for this, Ann."

"Then whom should I blame?" she shot back. "You couldn't wait to get away from here, so what the hell are you doing back?"

He blinked in surprise at her sudden change of tactics and at her use of such strong language—at least strong for her. Jack was right, he thought in fascination. She *had* changed. He couldn't help wondering how much. But obviously her negative feelings concerning him hadn't altered. It hurt him to see bitterness and contempt glittering in those lovely green eyes when there had once been love. So much love, and all wasted.

He turned away from her angry gaze.

"Can we talk about this? Reasonably?" he added as he stared pensively at the woods. "The situation in town could easily get out of hand, and this animosity between us only adds fuel to the fire."

"What did you expect, Drew?" Ann's temper blazed in sharp comparison to his calm tone. "That you could come back here after all these years, and I'd hand over the title of my farm to you without a word? That I'd let you uproot a whole town, *my* town, without a fight?"

"I was expecting—I was *hoping,*" he amended with emphasis, turning back to her, "that you'd at least be willing to listen."

"There's nothing you can say that will change my mind," Ann said stubbornly, folding her arms firmly across her chest. "I don't see that we have anything to talk about."

"Unfortunately, that's always been your attitude," Drew said with heated impatience. "You never thought what anyone else wanted was important. All you cared about was *your* feelings. What about the other people involved here? What about their feelings? Don't they count?"

"This is my land, and I have no intention of selling. I'm not trying to tell anyone else what to do with theirs," Ann said loftily, but the truth was she'd been miserable for months, wondering if she was doing the right thing.

"All right, forget about your own property for a moment. What about your council vote on the rezoning issue?

That doesn't affect your land one way or the other. Why are you so against it?"

Her chin tilted. "I'm doing what I think is best for the community."

His eyes narrowed. "Oh, I see. And you can determine that without even listening to what I or anyone else from my company have to say. Hasn't that self-righteous attitude worn a little thin over the years?"

Ann glared up at him, seeing him through a red mist. No one had ever been able to make her angrier faster than Drew Maitland. "I have good reason to be self-righteous where you're concerned. Or have you forgotten?"

"I haven't forgotten anything," Drew responded quickly, his own anger growing. "So if you want to take this little stroll down memory lane, let's remember who dumped who that summer. You didn't want me anymore."

"Because you tried to make me choose between you and my family!"

"I only tried to make you see what they were doing to you, to *us*. It irked me the way they used you, Ann. Both Adam and Aiden played you like a violin, and you let them because you thought it was your sacred duty to take care of them. Everything else, including me, had to take a backseat."

"You think that excuses what happened?" she asked bitterly, turning away from him.

Drew took a deep breath and let it out, the sound as loud as a steam engine in the dead silence between them. "I never tried to make excuses, I only tried to explain, to make you understand. You're a grown woman now. Surely you can understand how things might have gotten out of hand under the circumstances—"

"I may be a grown woman, Drew, but I've never been able to understand how you could have slept with my sister when you professed to love me."

He shoved a tired hand through the golden strands of his hair as he stood silently for a moment, his eyes remote, as though he was trying to distance himself from their conversation. "It always comes back to that, doesn't it?"

"You're damn right it does," Ann retorted, her green eyes glistening with contempt. "I've waited ten years to tell you exactly what I think of your *mistake* as you so euphemistically put it last night."

"Then say it," Drew said angrily. "Say it all, Angel. You can't tell me anything I haven't told myself a million times over. Yes, I made a mistake, but don't you make one in assuming I didn't pay for it. I paid for it all right. I paid for it with ten years of my life."

"And so did I," she said simply. "You made your choice, Drew. I didn't have one."

"We all have choices. I learned that lesson the hard way. You have a choice right now, Ann. You can let the past stay where it belongs, and we can start over, right here and now."

She looked at him incredulously. "Why should I want to do that? Because you're suddenly ready to start over? Because your job requires you to get along with me now?" She shook her head in disgust. "I think I resent you more now than I ever have."

He turned away from her, muttering an oath, then spun back around to face her. "Do you think this is healthy?" he asked in frustration. "You living with your bitterness and me with my guilt?"

"Guilt?"

"Of course I feel guilty," he said wearily, the anger suddenly draining away. "Did you think I wouldn't?"

"But—" Ann's gaze wandered toward the green expanse of the river, her own anger dissolving like the early morning mist, leaving her feeling drained and openly vulnerable somehow. "If you felt so guilty, why didn't you try to call me or see me after the divorce?"

He searched her face, his gaze deep and probing. Then he shuttered his expression. "I had my reasons."

"I'm sure you did," Ann replied caustically, studying his silent profile. Then, as if to herself, she said, "In ten long years, there wasn't one word from you."

"I did come to see you once," Drew said, his gaze still pensive. "Right after the divorce, I came out to L.A. to talk to you. I waited across the street from your apartment building for you to come home. I saw you and your...friend—" Hell, call him what he was, Drew mocked himself. Her *lover.* "I saw the two of you drive up and go into the building together." Would he ever forget that day? Forget that unknown man's possessive hand on Angel's back, the way he had smiled down at her, sharing secrets with her that Drew had never known.

"Why didn't you come in?"

He smiled slightly, but there was no humor in his voice when he answered. "I didn't think I'd be particularly welcome, an old boyfriend showing up out of the blue."

"David wouldn't have minded. He knew all about you."

David. So that was his name. Somehow putting a name to that face made Drew feel worse, made their relationship harder to deny. Envy, as he hadn't known it in years, suddenly rose up inside him, threatening the fragile control he'd fought to maintain for so long.

"If you told him about me, about us, then you must have trusted him a great deal."

There was only a slight hesitation before she answered, "I did."

"And loved him?" Drew found that he couldn't look at her anymore, did not want to see the answer in her eyes. He already felt as though someone had punched him, very hard, in the gut.

"Yes."

His eyes closed briefly. He thought he'd known pain, emptiness, but the emotions plunging through him now were razor-sharp, precise, slicing open wounds he knew would be a long time in healing. He wanted to ram his fist against the wooden post by his side, or into *David's* face. He wanted to grab Ann and make her tell him that she had been lying, that she had never loved anyone else.

Instead he said, very quietly, "I told myself when I first heard you were with someone that it was because I had hurt you so deeply you were on the rebound. I told myself you had made a mistake just as I had, and that it wouldn't last. I told myself a lot of things back then, but I never dreamed you'd fallen in love with someone else."

Tell him the truth, Ann commanded herself. *I didn't fall in love with David. I loved him as a friend, a companion, someone who helped me through the worst time of my life. I loved him, yes, but I wasn't* in *love with him. You ruined that for me forever. I could never love anyone the way I loved you.*

"You don't have to talk about it," Drew said softly, breaking the heavy silence between them. "In fact, I don't think I want to hear any more."

She cut her eyes back to him. "You were the one who wanted to get into all this, Drew. I was perfectly happy leaving things the way they were."

"I know," he said, frowning at the toe of his boot. "But no matter how . . . uncomfortable it may be, there are things we need to say to each other, things that have gone too long unsaid. We need to talk about—"

"Aiden."

A cold knot formed in the pit of Drew's stomach as he tried not to outwardly react to the name. But it was a name that would always be between them, and if they were ever to put the past behind them, they would have to deal with it, starting here and now. He took a long breath. "I never really knew the circumstances surrounding her death. Would you mind telling me?"

"I don't mind," she replied, but when she lifted her eyes to his, pain flickered in the soft, green depths. With an unconsciously graceful movement, she sank to the ground and drew her knees up, clasping her slender hands around them. She stared thoughtfully across the river as Drew sat down beside her. "I suppose I should have called you and told you myself when it happened, but I... couldn't."

She faltered again, dropping her gaze, and Drew wanted to stop her from going on, but he knew he couldn't. Not now. Not when this conversation might be the final cleansing they both needed.

"She'd gone with a group of people to some sort of private island off the coast of Cozumel for a midnight party. Evidently there was a lot of booze floating around. Everyone was pretty out of it. No one missed her until it was time to head back to the hotel. The last anyone had seen of her, she'd been going out for a swim. A search was conducted, of course, but they couldn't find her.

"I was contacted two days later by the Mexican authorities. She was missing, presumed drowned. The search went on for a few more days, but with the currents around the island, the authorities told me it was pretty hopeless. Jack flew down to try to keep the search going for as long as possible, but..." she trailed off, shrugging helplessly. "He recovered her personal effects from her hotel room and brought them home. Her wedding ring was among the jewelry she had with her. Would... you like to have it back?" Ann asked hesitantly.

"No!" Drew exploded, then realizing how he sounded, he tried to temper his words. "I'm sorry, Ann, but I don't want it. You keep it." *Or better yet, throw it away,* he thought bitterly.

Ann nodded briefly, her gaze not quite meeting his. "The rest you know," she concluded softly.

"Was she in Mexico on vacation?"

"As far as I know."

"I don't know if you were aware of this or not," Drew said slowly, measuring his words. "But Aiden was into gambling. She had a serious problem."

Ann stared at him in surprise. "Problem? I knew she liked to gamble. She and Jack used to meet in Las Vegas once or twice a year, but I'd hardly call that a problem."

"Ann... Aiden had a very addictive personality." *Pills, booze, you name it. Nothing was ever enough,* he thought bitterly, remembering acutely the agony she'd put them both through. He said softly, "She couldn't stop. I paid off her debts for years, even after the divorce. But there was never an end to it, and I finally had to say no the last time she came to me for help."

Ann was still looking at him as if she didn't quite believe him. "When was this?"

"About a month before she died."

"She called and asked me for money, too," Ann told him. Her words were calm, but her expression was rigid, as though she was trying very hard to hide her emotions. "She was still living in L.A., picking up an occasional acting job, mostly commercials. Neither one of us was able to touch our trust funds without Jack's okay, and evidently she couldn't convince him she really needed the money. I didn't have any money to give her, either, but I could have helped her out. I could have gotten the money somehow. I'll never forget the desperation in her voice when she hung up that day. I thought she was acting, Drew. She could be so convincing when she wanted to be. If only I'd known—" She broke off, then lifted her haunted eyes to meet Drew's. "That was the last time I talked to her."

"You never heard from her at all?"

Again a slight hesitation. "Not until the night she died. She contacted me then."

As their eyes met, Drew felt a slight tremor of dread course through him. "You're not talking by telephone, are you?"

"She was still reaching out to me," Ann said in a broken whisper. "I'd turned my back on her, and she was still reaching out to me, even at the end."

A deep helplessness settled over Drew. He felt powerless to fight this. He could see the guilt in her eyes, the deep sadness that creased her features. Now might be the right time to clue her in on a few basic truths concerning her sister, but he had no wish to cause her more pain. Besides, telling her the truth about Aiden wouldn't erase what he had done ten years ago. Nothing would do that.

He'd thought talking about Aiden, about her death, might somehow release them from the anguish of the past. But he could see now that he had been mistaken. Aiden would always be a part of both of them, an inescapable reminder. Even from her grave, she was still coming between them.

"Ann—" he began, but she had already turned away.

"I think we've both said enough for one day," she said.

"Maybe you're right," he agreed with a heavy sigh. He stood and stared down at her for a moment. "Goodbye, Ann." She looked up at him then. Her eyes were dry, but he could see the tears deep inside, even if she couldn't.

"Drew—"

"Yes?"

She paused for a moment, worrying her bottom lip with her teeth, as though torn by indecision. Finally she said softly, "Don't go back over that bridge."

He smiled sadly. "Don't worry. I'll take the long way home. I always have."

Except for periodic cleaning, her sister's room had been left untouched since the day Aiden had left home years ago. Ann stood in the doorway, her gaze roaming the elegant white, gold and crystal decor—so incongruent for a teenage girl's bedroom, yet so suited to Aiden.

Down the hall, her father's room remained the same as it had years ago. Ann hadn't intentionally kept them as shrines, but she wondered now if that had been her unconscious motive. Changing their rooms might somehow seem disloyal to them, as if she was trying to wipe away the memory of them in her life. Ann knew that was irrational thinking, but her feelings for her father and Aiden—especially Aiden—were too deep-rooted and complex for self-analysis. She only knew that this room disturbed her now in a way it never had before.

Ann took a tentative step inside. If she concentrated hard enough, she could almost see her sister sprawled across the satin bedspread, headphones covering her ears, a dozen fashion magazines spread around her. If she closed her eyes, she could almost smell the scent of Aiden's perfume, spicy and exotic. A crystal flacon of Shalimar still sat atop Aiden's dressing table, and inside the glass swan jewelry box was her wedding ring.

Ann crossed the room and picked up a glass-framed photograph from the dresser top. Light from the window sparked the edge of the crystal, reflecting dozens of tiny rainbows against her hands as she stood studying the photograph.

She and Aiden had just turned sixteen when the picture had been taken. Their arms were around each other as they stared into the camera—Aiden laughing, her long, red hair lifted away from her face by a stray breeze; and Ann, a paler, dimmer copy of her sister with her short cap of hair and her reserved smile.

Ann set the photograph down in distaste and turned away. Her gaze rested briefly on the crystal swan. Perhaps, she thought fleetingly as she moved toward the door, the time had come to start thinking about redecorating. Perhaps, just perhaps—she paused at the door and stared into the room for a moment—it might be time for some changes.

Then she left the room and closed the door behind her.

Four

The days slipped by, hot and humid and without so much as a sprinkle of rain to cool the air—or the tempers—as the debate raged on.

Drew had been in town two weeks and still Crossfield remained a town divided. For the past several days, most of his time had been occupied with meetings. The individuals and groups he'd spoken with had all treated him cordially, some even enthusiastically. Others gave indications of slowly coming around to seeing his point of view.

Earlier, Drew had had lunch with Bernice Ballard, Wilma Gates, and some of the other ladies of the Historical Society, whose primary concern was the preservation of several turn-of-the-century houses along the waterfront. Drew's suggestion for renovating the old houses for use as specialty shops and restaurants along a riverwalk had greatly appealed to the ladies. By the time lunch had ended, they'd all made plans to meet on Riverside Drive one day next week to discuss his plans further.

One on one, the meetings were going exceptionally well. But as a whole, the factions were even more bitterly discordant than they had been when the town council meeting had gotten so out of hand that first night. It was as though the development project was no longer the main issue, but a catalyst for differences in personalities, morals, life-styles and everything else to become the hub of conflict.

What concerned Drew most was the rash of vandalism in Crossfield in the past week. A couple of houses along the river had been defaced with spray paint, and the air had been let out of Wilma Gates's tires in the parking lot of the local discount store while she and Bernice were shopping.

The shots that had been fired on Ann's property the other day still nagged at him, too, although she had casually shrugged off the incident. Drew had taken it upon himself to speak with Sheriff Hayden, but he'd merely agreed with Ann's theory about poachers. That seemed the logical conclusion, Drew had to admit, but he still worried that Ann might be the target of the vandals. Something had to be done—and quickly—to stop the violence before it escalated beyond the point of pranks.

Sitting in the tiny office in city hall that the mayor had given him for the duration of his stay, Drew loosened his tie and yanked open the top button of his shirt. The tiny window unit air conditioner put out about twice as much noise as air. The office was like a sweatbox. He swiveled the cracked leather chair toward the opposite window and stared thoughtfully out into the shaded alley beyond.

Towering thunderclouds, dark and unmoving, piled up in the west as they had every afternoon for well over a week. But the rain remained elusive. The air crackled with electricity, and Drew suspected the mounting tension of the weather played an important role in the flare of tempers in town.

Just over a week until the vote, he thought gloomily, and Ann was doing everything in her power to avoid him. He hadn't seen nor heard from her since that morning he'd seen her at the river. He suspected she was hiding out, waiting for him to slowly sink into oblivion.

In a way, he could understand her wariness toward him. Facing the truth, admitting to himself that he still wanted her after all these years, had unsettled him, too. For years his life had been totally predictable, planned mostly around his work. Looking back now, he could see that his ambition, his quick rise up the corporate ladder, had been his own way of hiding, of running from the past that was still very painful to him.

But he'd known when he'd first seen Angel at Aiden's memorial service that his feelings for her were still with him, as deep and consuming as ever. So he'd gone back to Dallas, and made his pitch to his superiors concerning the location of Riverside Development's latest project; from that moment on, he'd been biding his time. Until now.

Drew tipped his chair back, and rested his head against the cracked leather. He might get kicked in the teeth one more time for trying what he was thinking, but he was tired of fighting his feelings, tired of the guilt, tired of wasting time.

He was just plain tired of waiting. And before this day was over, Angel would know it.

With new determination, he got up and strode out of the room, turning down the hall toward the council chambers. He smiled to himself. He hadn't felt this good in years.

Why was he smiling at her like that? Ann wondered nervously, toying with her pencil as Mayor Sikes presided over the council meeting. Ever since she'd walked into the room and taken her seat, Ann had been aware of some kind of current passing between her and Drew every time she looked up. His blue eyes were darkly intense each time he met her gaze, and his lips curved in a smile that could only be called enticing.

And Ann found she couldn't keep from glancing up again and again. Her heart began to hammer as they stared at each other across the table. Drew steepled his fingers beneath his chin and regarded her with smoldering admiration. The pulse in her throat throbbed, harder and faster, as his gaze slowly slid over her, caressing her every feature but lingering longest on her mouth.

Unconsciously, Ann's tongue darted out to moisten lips that had been dried by the heat of his stare. Drew's eyes narrowed. She saw him shift slightly in his chair, and her face flamed with the realization of what they had been doing.

"What do you think of the fireworks, Ann?"

"Wh-what?" Her gaze veered to the head of the table, where Mayor Sikes eyed her expectantly over the rim of his spectacles.

"The fireworks. What do you think of the fireworks?" he asked impatiently.

"I...like them," she said lamely.

Out of the corner of her eye, she saw Drew's mouth twitch, saw the amusement dancing in his blue eyes at her discomfort. Without quite knowing how it happened, she found herself speaking out in protest.

"But do you honestly think a picnic will fix what's wrong in this town? I've never seen Crossfield like this. You can hardly walk down the street without being caught up in an argument. I'm afraid the citizens of this town won't be pacified by a barbecue supper and a few firecrackers."

"If you have a better suggestion, we'd be glad to listen," Drew said quietly from the other side of the table. His voice, deep and sensual, sent a shiver of awareness flooding through her, threatening to strip her of the precious few defenses she'd managed to marshal since that day in the woods. She glanced toward him only to be caught once more by his intense gaze. He smiled openly, that slow, sexy smile she remembered only too well, and her heart thumped almost painfully against her chest.

She set her mouth in a firm line of defiance. "You could stop the development project," she offered. "Everything was fine until you. . . your company moved in here."

"If you call soaring unemployment and a stagnant economy fine," Drew countered, his tone still one of polite indulgence, which ruffled Ann's feathers even more.

"You tell her, Drew," Nate Bennett chimed in from the back of the room where he'd been sprawled in a folding metal chair listening to the meeting. Slowly he got to his feet, weaving slightly as he stared through bloodshot eyes at Ann. "I think a barbecue supper is a fine idea. No one around here ever turns down free eats. Might be just the ticket to loosen up a few of those uptight, closeminded, old biddies causing all the trouble. 'Course, I don't lump you in that category, Ann. You sure ain't old." His slightly out-of-focus gaze raked her up and down, bringing hot color to Ann's cheeks.

Drew felt his own blood start to boil at the insulting way Bennett was addressing Ann. He started to rise, but Mayor Sikes put a restraining hand on his shoulder.

"Nat, if that's all you have to add, why don't you go on out and call Wanda to come get you. I don't want to see you out on the road in your condition."

"Just tryin' to offer an opinion," Nate slurred, spreading his hands in the air in acquiescence. "One more thing I wanna get straight with Drew here. If Ann keeps refusing to sell, is that gonna mess up the deal for me and Sam McCauley, her property being right between ours and all?"

"I discussed this with you the other day, Nate," Drew said coolly, holding onto his temper by a thread. "The plans for the outlying properties have not yet been finalized. No deals have been made, and won't be, until I have the chance to speak with the property owners along the river and determine where we stand with all of them. That's the only answer I can give you right now."

Nate stood silently for a moment, looking as though he wanted to argue. Finally, with one last glare at Ann, he nodded and ambled out of the room, letting the door slam with a jarring bang behind him.

Ann sat down, feeling completely humiliated by Nate Bennett's open animosity. She could feel Drew's eyes on her, and the color rose to her face once more under his scrutiny. But she wouldn't look up. She wouldn't give him the satisfaction of seeing how upset she really was. She would do nothing to make him think he had the upper hand.

"You'd better ride out and talk to him tomorrow, Drew," Mayor Sikes advised, staring at Drew over the rim of his bifocals. "He could get to be a real problem. He's seeing dollar signs every time he starts drinking, and I don't want him causing any trouble. Talk to him, see if you can pacify him for a while. I want this project to succeed as much as anyone, but I don't condone what's been going on around here."

"Neither do I," Drew said, his mouth a hard, grim line. "I'll see what I can do."

The meeting went on for a few minutes longer, but as soon as Mayor Sikes adjourned, Ann made ready her escape. Drew got up, too, his purpose abundantly clear as he started around the table toward her.

"Hold on there a minute, Drew. I need to talk to you before you skedaddle."

Ann was already at the door when she heard Mayor Sikes waylay Drew. She looked back, and for a moment, their gazes clashed. Drew smiled slightly, letting her know that she might have won the battle but the war was far from over. She turned and made good her retreat.

Ann emerged from the steamy bathroom and sat down on the side of her bed as she smoothed lotion onto her damp skin. The movement of her hand slowed as she looked up with a frown. There was a noise, a tiny *poing* against her bedroom window. At first she thought she had imagined the sound, but there it was again, louder this time, as though something had been tossed insistently against the pane.

She crossed the room and stood staring down at the garden for a moment before shoving up the sill. All was still and silent below. The air was hot and thick and heavy with the fragrance of flowers, and the trees and bushes in the garden were motionless.

The stars were out, thousands and thousands as only a country sky can boast. They cast a muted glow among the topiary, and it took Ann a few seconds to realize that one of the shadows had moved.

Her heart leaped to her throat as she stood staring down at the dark silhouette that moved into the strip of light spilling from her window. "Drew?"

"I didn't wake you, did I? I saw your light was still on." His features were dark and indistinct in the faint light. "I rang the bell a couple of times, but I guess you didn't hear it."

"I was in the shower." She paused, biting her bottom lip. "What are you doing here?"

"I need to talk to you. Could I come in for a minute?"

"I'll come down," she said quickly, turning away from the window and realizing for the first time that she'd been standing in the window, backlighted by her bedroom light, wearing nothing but a bath towel. She grabbed a pink silk robe from her closet and whipping off the towel, quickly belted the robe around her waist. The soft fabric billowed around her legs as she dashed down the stairs and across the foyer.

Drew met her at the front door, and the only thing that stood between them for a moment was the screen door. But even that shield was gone when Ann pushed it open and stepped out onto the porch.

"What are you doing all the way out here this time of night?" she asked again as she moved a few steps away from him and perched on the edge of the porch railing.

"I happened to be in the neighborhood," he said with a grin, leaning his shoulder against a post. At her dubious look, he held up three fingers. "Scout's honor."

"You were never a Boy Scout, Drew."

"Maybe I should have been," he said ironically. "Look, I'm sorry about the way Bennett acted earlier at the meeting. I just came from his place. I don't think you'll be having any more trouble from him."

Ann frowned slightly. "I appreciate that, but you don't have to fight my battles for me. I'm a grown woman."

I gave up looking for heroes a long time ago. Her bitter words that first night came floating back to Drew, leaving him with a curious feeling of regret.

"You're definitely a grown woman," he said softly, letting his gaze linger over her. The silky fabric of her robe clung to her curves, molding her exact shape in a way that was far more erotic than any flimsy bit of lingerie could ever be. He could see just a hint of leg where the material separated at the bottom, just a shadow of cleavage where it joined at the top. But it was enough to leave him wondering whether or not she wore anything underneath.

The scent of her perfume, a light, flowery, thoroughly provocative fragrance, seemed to emanate from the very essence of her. She tossed her head slightly, and starlight rippled through her hair.

"Was that the only reason you drove out here?" Ann asked bluntly, doing her best to break the spell.

"No." He paused for a moment, his eyes never leaving her face. "As a matter of fact, I came to ask you to dinner."

"Dinner? I'm not sure that's a good idea." Ann's frown deepened as she shifted on the railing. The slit in her robe slid higher, drawing Drew's gaze like a bee to honey.

Reluctantly he lifted his eyes. "It's a great idea. I've had lunch or dinner, breakfast or tea with almost everybody in town except you. How can I ever convince you of my good intentions if you won't talk to me?"

A pool of light spilled from the front window and highlighted a moth that clung to the screen. Ann let her gaze focus on that rather than on Drew. "I'm not sure you can do that anyway," she said finally.

"You'll never know unless you hear me out, will you? As an elected official, it's your duty—"

"I wasn't elected," she corrected him dryly. "Mayor Sikes convinced me to serve the rest of my father's term. He neglected to tell me, until I'd already agreed to serve, that Dad had just been elected to another six-year term. I still have four more years to go."

"You could always resign."

"No, I couldn't. I made a promise—"

It was a struggle, an almost superhuman feat, to keep the exasperation from his tone. She had always been so damned single-minded. Drew permitted himself only a tiny sigh. "And you always keep your promises, I know. So why not promise to have dinner with me? I would really like to see you."

"About business?"

He paused only marginally. "Of course. I'm driving back to Dallas tomorrow night, but we could have an early dinner. I'll pick you up at six."

"I haven't said I'd go," Ann reminded him quickly, but she could feel herself weakening. His voice was like liquid velvet, warm and soft, flowing over her in a seductive wash of textures and feelings. "It's late. I'm going in now," she said in a rush as she stood and made to brush by him. His hand shot out and caught her arm.

"Not quite yet."

She stiffened beneath his touch as her heart began to hammer in earnest, shortening her breath. The heat from his touch sent rays of excitement spiraling through her. His hands moved up her arms, grasping her shoulders as he held her before him. Their gazes locked in combat, but Ann could feel the onslaught of desire threatening her defenses. The walls were crumbling around her heart with every moment they stood so near.

Oh, God, how could this be? she despaired inwardly. How could she despise him and want him at the same time? After everything he had done to her, how could she crave with a near physical ache, the touch of his hands against her skin, the caress of his lips against her own? He had chosen her sister over her. He had married Aiden. She should want nothing from this man.

She wanted everything from him.

She moaned softly, the sound astonishingly clear in the silent darkness. She heard Drew's sharp intake of breath just before he pulled her to him, crushing her against his chest. His lips touched her hair, her eyes, her nose, her chin, and then finally, briefly, her mouth.

"Ann, Ann, don't you see?" he whispered with an edge of desperation in his voice. His hand gently smoothed back errant wisps of her hair. "It's not me you're fighting. You're fighting yourself."

"That's not true," she denied weakly, closing her eyes against the raging tremors in her stomach. His finger outlined her lips, a touch so sensuous Ann felt herself sway into him. Her breasts were flattened against his chest. She could feel the tingling awareness in the sensitive tips, longed to move them against him, letting the delicious friction drive the ache deeper and deeper within her.

But she held herself still in his arms, still and unyielding as a tide of emotion threatened to carry her away.

"Let go, Ann," Drew murmured against her ear, letting his tongue flick out to moisten her lobe. "Let yourself feel what your body's trying to tell you."

"I don't feel anything," she denied, the quiver in her voice betraying her vow.

"Don't you?" His breath, warm and urgent, feathered against her skin, causing prickles of sensation along the delicate column of her back. She shivered in his arms, feeling them immediately tighten around her. "I can feel your heart pounding," he said softly, sliding one hand between them to splay it against her left breast. "I can feel you trembling." His thumb wove an erotic pattern around the hardened nipple, so seductively prominent beneath the layer of silk. "I can feel your desire."

He groaned softly as she responded to his touch. His thumb continued the magic while he pressed his hips against her, letting her feel the hardness of his own desire.

His tongue rimmed her lips, teasing, tormenting, then slid inside her mouth, grazing the edges of her teeth, probing deep, deeper, until he forced hers to reciprocate. His mouth ground against hers in a kiss that was far less gentle than any she'd ever known from him, and far more provocative. It was the kiss of a stranger and yet its familiarity was an erotic stimulation, a drug that lulled her senses and promised her a forbidden paradise.

"Drew, don't," she pleaded when he lifted his mouth from hers to rain hot, liquid kisses along her neck. "Please. This isn't right."

He paused, raising his head to look down at her. His eyes were dark and heavy, smoldering with barely leashed passion. But there was also a spark of anger there, and that was the emotion that caused Ann to shudder.

"I'm making it right," he said darkly, his gaze reckless and daring. "I want to see you again. Tomorrow night."

It was a command, not a request this time, and Ann felt her defenses regrouping in protest. "I can't."

Drew stared down at her, his hands moving to grasp her arms as he held her in front of him. "Can't or won't?"

"Maybe I already have plans," she said angrily, jerking her arms from his grasp.

"Then you can change them for me. You can't hide from me forever, Ann. I'll pick you up at six."

"No! I mean...I'll meet you at the restaurant," Ann conceded grudgingly.

Drew's eyes narrowed on her as he moved toward her. "Can I trust you to be there?"

"You've no reason to distrust me," Ann said innocently, but they both knew her words were laced with a double entendre.

Drew gave her a tight, little smile that had nothing to do with mirth. His head dipped toward hers as he said in a low, threatening voice, "That's right, I don't. And besides, if you don't show, I'll come looking for you."

Before she could object, he lowered his head, swiftly capturing her lips in a steamy, illicit kiss that aroused Ann to a fevered desperation beyond her wildest imaginings.

Angel? Angel?

Ann moaned softly as her head thrashed against the pillow. A cold draft tripped along her skin, causing her to shiver in her sleep. She tried to pull the cover on her bed higher, but her hands were numb, lifeless.

You know, don't you, Angel?

I don't know what you're talking about, Aiden. Know what?

You know who Drew sees when he looks into your eyes. He sees me.

That's not true! You're lying!

Have I ever lied to you, Angel? Why else do you think he's come back to you after all these years? He's looking for me.

Ann's eyes flew open, staring wildly into the darkness as a scream rose in her throat. Her heart slammed against her chest as she lifted a hand to her face, feeling the cold, clamminess of her own skin.

A dream.

It had been a dream. She was sure of it now as her surroundings slowly came into focus in the surreal half light of the moon. She gasped as a sudden movement at the window caught her eye. The curtains billowed ghostlike in the distorted light, their shape suspended for a moment by the mild breeze that stirred them.

On the nightstand by her bed, the clock told her in electric blue neon that it was nearly three in the morning. Hours since she'd seen Drew.

Ann slid back down against the pillows, but she didn't close her eyes. Drew had come back, after all these years, and he'd brought the nightmares with him....

Five

The next evening Ann stood inside Donna Cooper's hospital room and dialed the number for the Crossfield Motel. Her heart gave an unexpected twist when she was connected through to Drew's room and his voice sounded across the line.

"Drew, it's Ann."

"Hi, honey. Are you already at the restaurant? I was just about to leave—"

Ann missed the rest of his sentence because she'd pulled the receiver away from her ear. She stared at it. Honey? She put it back to her ear and quickly said, "I'm not at the restaurant. I'm at the hospital."

"Hospital? Are you hurt? Sick? What happened?"

The concern in his voice was so genuine, guilt stabbed at Ann for what she was about to do. She dashed it away, telling herself she had no other choice. Her friend needed her. "I'm okay, but Donna Cooper's here. I dropped by to see her a little while ago, and she started having contractions. Wayne's out of town so I drove her to the hospital."

"Is she all right?"

"The doctor says it was false labor, but he's keeping her in the hospital overnight. I—I just don't think she should be alone right now. This is her first baby, and both of us were pretty scared earlier."

"I see." Disappointment was obvious in his voice, but so was his concern. "Would you like me to come over?"

"That's not necessary, but I appreciate the offer. I'm... sorry about dinner."

"So am I. I'll call you when I get back. Take care of yourself, Ann, and give Donna my best."

"I will. And, Drew? Thanks for understanding."

"You bet. See you in a few days."

Ann hung up the phone slowly, wondering if the strange little fluttering in her stomach was relief or remorse. With a heavy sigh, she turned to face Donna, who was glowering at her from her hospital bed.

"Why did you do that?"

Ann gave an indifferent little shrug as she sat down on the edge of Donna's bed. "What?"

"What? *What?* Break your date with Drew, that's what. The doctor said I'm perfectly fine. I'll be out of here in the morning."

"Well, I just thought you might need me," Ann said defensively. "Besides, it wasn't a date."

"Excuse me, but didn't he ask you to have dinner with him? And didn't you say yes? That's what most people call a date."

"Well, this was just business," Ann insisted.

Donna's dark brows lifted over her brown eyes, flashing Ann a "give me a break" look. Ann started to protest again, but knew it would do no good at all. Her friend was a hopeless romantic, always had been and always would be. Ever since Drew had come back to town, she'd been dropping hints right and left of a fairy-tale ending for the long, lost lovers.

But, of course, she and Drew had never really been lovers, and not for the first time in the last ten years, Ann felt a keen stab of regret over the loss of something she had never had.

"Of course, I haven't even seen him yet," Donna was saying as Ann forced her attention back to her friend. "But Kelly told me she and Jack had lunch with him the other day. She said he looked wonderful." Donna laughed ruefully as she folded her hands on top of her generous stomach. "Actually, she said he looked positively gorgeous and if Jack hadn't been there, she would've been drooling all over the place."

"That sounds like something your sister would say," Ann commented dryly.

"He always was positively gorgeous," Donna continued, eyeing Ann knowingly. "I used to think he and Jack were such hunks in high school. You and I were the envy of every girl in town. I never can pass the drive-in without remembering how the four of us used to double date all the time."

"That was all a long time ago," Ann said softly, looking down at her hands.

"Oh, I know," Donna agreed off-handedly. "But those old memories don't go away, and sometimes it's kind of fun to reminisce. Both Jack and Drew were such hell-raisers back then, but with you, Drew was so different, so...tender. Jack, on the other hand, was always a rascal. He never cared about anything except what *Jack* wanted. We had more fights about s-e-x. At least until I gave in, that is."

Ann's eyes widened in surprise as she stared at her friend. "I never knew you and Jack—that you—"

"Slept with him? It wasn't something I wanted to broadcast, particularly not to you. You always had such rigid ideals about that. I never told you this, but I was very en vious of the way Drew treated you, with such tenderness and respect, never pressuring you into something you weren't ready for. Back then I think I saw him as some sort of knight in shining armor."

Ann gave a small brittle laugh. "So did I until I found out what he really was."

"I think I admired him all the more after that because he was man enough to do the right thing," Donna said stubbornly. Then, impatiently, "Oh, don't look at me that way. I know what happened was wrong and I felt terrible for the way you were hurt. But Drew was hurt, too. You're the one who dumped him, remember? You wanted no part of the life *he* wanted. You disapproved of his friends, his life-style, even his plans for the future. You made him think he wasn't good enough for you."

"I never said that," Ann cried in protest. "I never even thought it."

"But Drew did."

"How do you know?" Ann asked suspiciously.

"Because he told me. He was hurt and lonely—and vulnerable, I imagine, since you and he didn't...I mean...well, he was a normal, healthy young man and...and..."

"And he wasn't getting sex from me."

"Well, yes. And Aiden had persuasions of her own she didn't mind using. It's not at all hard for me to visualize the scenario that night after you two broke up—"

"I'm afraid I've never been able to write it off so easily," Ann interrupted bitterly, averting her gaze from Donna's probing one.

"Don't you think it's time you did?" Donna asked softly. "I know you still have feelings for him. I can see it in your eyes every time his name's mentioned."

Ann hesitated, wanting to deny Donna's claim, but unable to. "I don't know what I feel," she finally admitted in a low, defeated voice. "How can I still feel anything for him? It's been *ten* years, Donna."

"From what I hear, I'd say those feelings are not one-sided. Drew has them, too, doesn't he?"

Ann sighed deeply, rubbing her forehead with the tips of her fingers, as though she could push away those unwanted emotions. "I don't know," she said in confusion, her green eyes misting as she stared at Donna. "But what difference does it make what either of us are or aren't feeling? There's too much bad road behind us. Too many things have happened." Her voice broke slightly as she dropped her gaze. "Aiden will always be between us."

"Aiden's dead," Donna said with a frown.

Ann shook her head sadly. "It doesn't matter. I'd always wonder..."

"Wonder what?"

Ann bit her lip, the urge to confide her secret feelings almost unbearable. But there was no way Donna could understand the complexity of her emotions. Ann wasn't sure she understood them herself. She shrugged dismissively. "It just wouldn't work. Besides, when his job's completed here, he'll be moving on. I'm sure he can't wait to get out of here and back to the city. He must be bored out of his mind in Crossfield, and I'm not up to keeping an old flame entertained for just a few nights." *No matter how many sparks are left,* she added silently.

"Dallas isn't that far away," Donna insisted, refusing to be daunted by Ann's objections. "If you decide to sell the farm, you might want to move to the city yourself."

Ann stared at her in astonishment. "I've no intention of selling the farm. It's my home."

"Haven't you ever heard the expression 'home is where the heart is'?" her friend asked in exasperation. "We both know you're hanging onto that old place because of the promise you made to your father. But he's dead, Ann, and so is Aiden. You have to think about yourself now. That land is worth a fortune. You could be set for life."

"Has Jack been talking to you?" Ann asked suspiciously. "He's been bullying me to sell for months now, but that land is mine," she said stubbornly. "I won't allow Drew to come in here and tear down everything—"

"And that's the real problem, isn't it?" Donna asked perceptively. "It's not the development project you're saying no to. It's Drew."

"I was opposed to that project before I even knew Drew was involved," Ann pointed out angrily. "And for your information, that's exactly why we were meeting tonight—to discuss Riverside's plans. I don't know how I can be any more fair than that."

"Don't you?"

Ann whirled at the masculine voice behind her. Drew's presence dominated the doorway. He stood with his left shoulder propped against the door frame while he held a huge bouquet of apricot roses in his right hand. The gleaming white walls accentuated the dark gray of his suit, the deep bronze of his skin, the vibrant blue of his eyes. Ann's hand fluttered to her throat in dismay.

"Drew! How wonderful to see you!" Donna exclaimed, ignoring the long, silent exchange between Drew and Ann. "Are those for me? Aren't you sweet!"

For one brief second, Ann thought Drew looked slightly taken aback. Then he grinned, making her stomach somersault with excitement, as he crossed the room and handed the flowers to Donna. "Of course, they're for you. How are you feeling?"

"Oh, I'm fine. I'll be out of here in the morning. First baby jitters, the doctor called it. Wasn't it nice of Ann to stay and keep me company?"

"Very nice," Drew said, letting his gaze slide to Ann, telling her with the slight tilt of his brow that he knew exactly why she had stayed. His eyes reflected a subtle warning as if to say, "See? I told you I'd come looking for you."

"It was a little more than jitters," Ann murmured, contritely lowering her eyes. "You were having contractions."

"I know," Donna agreed, the sparkle in her eyes displaced by worry. "I *was* scared. This baby means so much to both Wayne and me, I don't know what he would do if anything happened."

"Ann said Wayne's out of town. Have you called him?" Drew asked softly.

Donna bit her lip as the furrows in her brow deepened. "No. I didn't see any need to worry him. I know he'd drive right back home, and then I'd be worried about him on the road worrying about me."

"Call him," Drew said, his tone quietly insistent. "He'll want to know."

He exchanged a careful glance with Ann, and she knew immediately what he was thinking because she was thinking it herself. The night Aiden had lost her baby, Drew had been out of town. He'd been in Dallas interviewing for the job with Braeden Industries. He hadn't known about the miscarriage until he got back to their apartment in Austin a few days later. No one had known until Aiden had called her father in near hysterics, and Adam in turn had called Ann. But several days had passed before Ann could bring herself to call her sister.

At the time, she had been so consumed by her own jealousy and guilt, Ann hadn't stopped to consider how Drew must have felt. Aiden had told her on the phone the baby had been a boy. Drew's son. He would be almost ten years old now....

She lifted her eyes to meet Drew's steady gaze, and it shook her to realize what she was feeling for him was compassion. Her knees trembled with the revelation because that one tender emotion paved the way for a thousand more stampeding over her, faster and stronger than the barricade she fervently kept trying to rebuild.

"Maybe you're right," Donna was saying slowly, drawing Drew's reluctant gaze. "I didn't think about it that way, but I probably should call him." She caught his hand and held it tightly in both of hers for a moment. "Thanks, Drew."

"For what? Not minding my own business?" he said with a grin.

"For still being such a good friend after all these years," Donna said warmly. "You haven't changed, you know."

"I have and I haven't," he said with a small, enigmatic smile as he turned toward Ann. "I wonder if you'd mind walking out with me, Ann? There's something I'd like to discuss with you before I hit the road."

Ann threw a distress signal to Donna, who summarily ignored it with a wave of her hand. "Go ahead. I want to call Wayne anyway."

She could hardly refuse, especially considering Donna was already dialing the phone. With a curt nod, she walked out of the room ahead of him.

The night was still and cloudless, with the day's heat still rising from the paved parking lot. Ann paused on the concrete steps outside the brightly lit entrance to let Drew take the lead. His arm caught her elbow, automatically and unconsciously, as he guided her toward his car.

The Jaguar gleamed darkly beneath the purplish glow of the overhead lights that lit the parking area. The lines were sleek and classic and slightly dangerous-looking—like the man who drove it. Ann let her eyes roam admiringly over the car, reluctant to make the transference to Drew.

"Like it?" he asked, smiling at her silence as he stood leaning against the door, arms folded across his chest.

Ann lifted her gaze to meet his. "It's gorgeous," she said honestly, her eyes slipping inadvertently over the familiar contours of his face.

"Would you like to go for a ride? I'd be happy to take you home," he suggested hopefully.

"Thanks, but I have my own car. Besides, I want to stay with Donna awhile longer." She paused, her eyes flickering up to meet his. "She's putting on a brave front, but she was really terrified earlier. I don't know if you know this or not, but she's had two miscarriages in the last three years. If anything happens to this baby—"

Drew's hand reached out and touched her arm. "She'll be all right, Ann."

The warmth of his touch was like a blanket of comfort. She wanted to wrap herself in it, snuggle against it, and forget all her cares and worries. The man who could so easily drive her to a blazing, consuming passion could also soothe her with just a soft word or a mere touch.

Ann swallowed hard against the lump that had suddenly formed in her throat. "I—I had to stay with her."

"Ann," his deep voice drew her gaze like a magnet. "I understand."

"So do I," she said softly, her voice trembling slightly. "Finally. Drew, I'm so sorry for what happened to your baby. Yours and Aiden's. I should have told you that a long time ago, but I couldn't bring myself to talk about it... It must have been horrible for you both."

Drew's gaze slipped away from hers. He stared, unseeing, at the rows of cars lining the parking lot. How could he tell her about that night or any other night he'd spent with her sister? How could he tell her about the lies, the threats, the constant torment his life had been? How could he tell her the reason that he'd stayed with Aiden for so long was because she'd tried to commit suicide twice when he'd walked out on her? How could he tell her that, when he couldn't bring himself to care anymore what happened to Aiden, she'd threatened him with something even more dire? Ann had a right to know everything, but God help him, he couldn't bring himself to tell her just how sick her sister had been. He'd taken so much from her already. Telling her the truth now would probably seem like one more betrayal to her.

His features were stark and sharpened by the strange light, the grooves around his mouth deep and harshly defined. He looked, not old of course, but somehow aged, with the wisdom of hard-learned lessons etched relentlessly on his face. For the first time Ann became aware of just how thin *his* defenses were. He'd accused her of living in the past, but obviously he had memories of his own he hadn't dealt with.

Why were they doing this to each other? Ann wondered in despair. Why were they torturing each other with memories when it was so much easier to pretend there was never anything to remember?

How much better to have let things simply drift along, destiny spinning her life one day at a time until the past, present and future were irrevocably woven together, one thread inseparable from the rest. How much easier to look back from a distance and view their lives—hers and Drew's and even Aiden's as that of characters in some ancient, passion-driven tragedy where lost love and betrayal were romanticized in poetry and love songs. How much easier to continue her life in the safe, cloaking mists of what might have been rather than face the bright reality of what was—the waiting, the uncertainty, the years of killing loneliness.

The same thought passed across Drew's features and with it, an almost instant denial. He stared at her, his features set with new resolve. "Can I call you when I get back?"

"When will that be?" Ann asked, dodging the question. She let her gaze focus on the red flash of the emergency room light. It seemed like a garish stage prop for the drama unfolding between her and Drew.

"By the end of the week. Certainly before the Fourth." He hesitated for a moment, as though unsure how to proceed. He said slowly, "You may have already heard this, but if not, I'd like to be the one to tell you. Mayor Sikes has asked me to speak at the barbecue. I'll be giving some specific details about Riverside's future plans."

Ann cut her eyes back to his. "He called me this morning," she said calmly. "What *you* may not know is that he also asked me to speak. I'll also be giving some specific details about Riverside's future plans."

Drew's brows shot up in surprise. When he spoke, his voice sounded oddly excited. "A debate?" He appeared to consider the notion for a moment, then he flashed her a quick grin with a hint of the old devilry. "Winner take all?"

Six

"How much have I missed?" Ann asked as she hurriedly took a seat in the stands next to Donna Cooper and her sister, Kelly. Ann had been working on her speech all morning and had completely forgotten about the annual Fourth of July softball game between Crossfield and their arch rivals, Crystal Falls.

"Almost all of it," Donna grumbled, keeping her gaze trained on the field. "It's the top of the ninth, they have two outs, two men on, and they're leading by one. Where've you been, anyway?" she asked in a slightly accusatory tone.

"Working." Ann turned her own attention to the field, quickly scanning the players. Jack was pitching, Wayne Cooper was playing first, Nathan Bennett second—

The loud *whack* of cowhide connecting with wood brought her attention back to home plate, then upward where the high, arcing ball headed for deep center field.

Beside her, Ann heard Donna and Kelly catch their breath as the ball began its downward arch. The center fielder, in jeans and a white T-shirt, took several running steps backward, his head tilted upward, his eyes on the ball. With an easy, graceful movement, he made a leaping catch, and the crowd in the stands went wild.

Donna and Kelly were laughing and clapping and hugging each other excitedly, but Ann had gone suddenly quiet as she watched the center fielder jogging toward the dugout.

A stray puff of arid wind caught the brim of her hat and snatched it from her head. Like a fiery veil, her hair spilled across her shoulders and down her back. Behind her, two preschoolers shouted and shrieked as they dashed for her spinning hat, but Ann didn't notice. Her eyes never left the tall, muscular figure entering the dugout. Slowly her hand lifted to remove her sunglasses.

Donna squeezed her arm excitedly. "Now that's more like it!" she said with satisfaction. "I knew he could do it!"

"He—"

Donna grinned smugly. "Drew, of course."

Drew! And she hadn't even known he was back! Obviously calling her hadn't been one of his priorities. She told herself it didn't matter in the least, but she couldn't help feeling slightly deflated as she watched him take a seat in the dugout.

"I didn't remember Drew Maitland being so hot!" Kelly added conspiratorially as she leaned around her sister to speak to Ann.

"Maybe that's because you were only a kid when he left town, and a tomboy at that," Donna remarked dryly.

"I can't imagine I was ever that much of a tomboy..."

Their conversation droned on, but Ann was only vaguely aware of it. Her eyes were inexorably drawn to the wire mesh dugout where she could see Drew sitting at the end of the bench, one knee drawn up while he watched the game. He'd taken off his cap, and a lock of dark gold hair fell across his forehead. He looked young and strong and capable, and something echoed in her mind—a memory or a dream that lingered and haunted, and suddenly her anger slipped away.

It might have been yesterday…except it wasn't. The time was the present, here and now, and Ann was feeling an odd excitement in the pit of her stomach, the kind she'd gotten years ago when she'd watched Drew play ball.

The first Crossfield batter flied out to loud cheering from the Crystal Falls' bleachers. The second batter, Nate Bennett, struck out. Angrily, he slung the bat away as he stomped off the field, flipping a one-finger salute to the visitors' stand, where the jeers and catcalls grew even louder. They were already dancing in the stands in anticipation of their eighth consecutive victory.

Ann sat quietly, her gaze following Drew as he moved to the on-deck circle. He selected a bat and took a couple of practice swings. The stretchy fabric of his T-shirt tightened over his arms and along his shoulders as his muscles boldly responded to the action. Ann felt something awaken inside her, an awareness that she had fought so hard to deny. She only had to close her eyes to remember the images of heaven she'd once found in those arms.

Reluctantly she tore her gaze away and tried to focus on Jack, who stood at the plate.

"Come on, baby, do it for me!" Kelly shouted, her voice easily carrying over the dull roar of the crowd.

Jack took the first pitch and sliced the ball neatly between the shortstop and the third baseman, then easily rounded first to land on second. The crowd in the Crossfield stands was ecstatic, especially Kelly as she jumped to her feet, screaming and applauding.

The action in the bleachers was suddenly as hot as that on the field, with the taunts and insults between the opposing fans becoming more and more graphic with each passing minute.

One man on, two outs, bottom of the ninth and trailing by one. That was the situation that faced Drew as he stepped to the plate and stooped to grit his hands with dirt.

It's just a game, he reminded himself as he turned to face the Crystal Falls' pitcher. But he knew it wasn't. Crossfield was hungry for a win. That win now depended on him, and, except for that one catch, he hadn't been playing worth a damn all day.

Hell, he didn't know what he was doing here in the first place. He'd come out to the ballpark earlier with the mayor to watch the game and had suddenly found himself on the field. The only good thing about the whole fiasco was that Ann hadn't shown up to witness his lackluster performance.

Every time Crossfield had been at bat, he'd searched the stands for her, remembering how she'd never missed one of his games when they were in high school. Back then she'd been his biggest fan, and she could make him feel ten feet tall, just by being there rooting for him. He'd always told her she was his inspiration when he played well, his consolation prize when he played poorly.

Times change, he thought, feeling a keen sense of loss.

The first ball was low and inside, but he swung anyway, his concentration completely lost.

"Strike one!" the umpire yelled behind him.

Patience! Drew commanded himself angrily. *Wait for it!* God, if he'd learned anything in the last ten years, it should be that.

The next ball curved to the outside and he let it go by.

"Strike two!"

He whirled in disbelief. "That ball was outside a mile!"

"Strike two, batter," the umpire told him blandly.

Ann watched the exchange with her heart in her throat. *It's just a game,* she reminded herself. But she knew it wasn't. The crowd was screaming in both stands. The Crossfield fans and players were counting on Drew to pull the game out. If he couldn't do it, Ann knew his pride would take a bashing. It might be just a game, but she knew he was taking it seriously.

"You can do it, Drew!"

The voice, *her* voice, registered with Drew just as he saw the ball leave the pitcher's hand. He swung hard, and the moment he felt the resistance against the bat, he knew the ball was gone.

Pandemonium was the order of the day as he rounded the bases and crossed home plate. The whole team was waiting to congratulate him. After seven years of famine, Crossfield had finally harvested a win. The celebration was going to be a long and hard one, judging by the collective jubilation of both players and fans.

The crowd streamed from the bleachers and surrounded them as they walked off the field. Someone had backed a pickup truck near the bleachers and sat a cooler on the tailgate. Ice cold beers were being passed all around amid gales of both feminine and masculine laughter.

Someone tapped Drew on the arm and he looked around and then down to find a sandy-haired, freckle-faced boy of ten or eleven staring up at him. Gravely the boy held out a scuffed softball to Drew.

"What's this?" Drew asked, holding out his hand to accept the ball.

"It's yours. I climbed over the fence and found it," the kid told him. He grinned suddenly, his eyes squinting almost closed in the bright sunlight. "It'll bring you luck."

"Thanks," Drew said, turning the ball over in his hand. "I'd say it already has." He tousled the boy's hair, and the grin grew even broader before he turned and tore away to join his friends.

"Hey, Drew, my main man," Jack said as he ambled up to Drew and threw a careless arm across his shoulders. "This one's for you."

Drew accepted the cold beer with a grateful grin. He lifted the bottle to his mouth, then halted the movement in mid-air.

Angel was standing at the bottom of the bleachers away from the rest of the crowd, and Drew caught his breath. This was the first time he'd seen her with her hair down, and the sight was magnificent, almost mystical, like a flaming halo framing her face. Her eyes were misty green and softly glowing as her gaze connected with his from a distance.

He'd often thought that if he could see Angel look at him that way one more time, if he could be her hero again for just one second, he could die a happy man.

At that moment, though, the last thing he thought about was dying. He'd never felt more alive. He could climb mountains, swim oceans to keep that special look on her face.

But what he really wanted to do, Drew realized, feeling the heat rush through his body, was to take her down to the river, where it was cool and shaded, and undress her slowly and adoringly, make love to her until ten years of loneliness had all faded away.

Something in his eyes must have revealed his inner thoughts for Angel's face altered. Her eyes softened even more and a blush touched her cheeks. And then she smiled at him.

He returned her smile, feeling more confident than he had in years. He'd just hit a game-saving home run with his best girl cheering in the stands and *damn* he felt good. The last ten years, all the anger and bitterness, the aching throb in his right shoulder were all minor details. This was a moment to savor.

"Drew! Congratulations! That was some hit!" Mayor Sikes parted the crowd around Drew and blustered his way through, his fat legs a splash of stark white between the hem of his plaid shorts and the top of his dark socks. He grabbed Drew's hand and pumped it fiercely, forcing Drew's attention toward him. "You just may have picked us up a few brownie points with that home run."

"Thanks, Mayor, but I doubt anyone will change their minds because of a ball game."

"You never can tell," Mayor Sikes insisted, clapping Drew soundly on the back. "You never can tell. Yessiree, things are looking good. Plenty of good food and drink for tonight, folks excited over the game, the weather holding in our favor, and you saving the day with a spectacular home run." He grinned broadly, winking at Drew as he rocked back and forth on his heels. "Perfect night for a few fireworks, eh, Drew?"

My sentiments exactly, Drew thought as he turned back to the bleachers. But Angel had already slipped away like an elusive dream.

Ann sat motionless in her car as she stared down at the picture in her hands. When she'd first seen the folded piece of paper lying in the front seat of her car, she'd thought it a piece of trash. Completely preoccupied with her disturbing thoughts of Drew, she'd opened it up and stared at it for a moment before the impact fully hit her. Someone was sending her a message.

The page looked as though it had been ripped from some sort of old religious book. The graphic scene depicted a fallen angel, her face contorted in agony, as she lay chained to the surface of a burning lake. The flames surrounding her leaped closer and closer.

As Ann stared at the picture, she could almost feel the fiery heat, the writhing agony as the angel struggled to escape destruction. The picture was both beautiful and horrible, a scene that attracted even as it repelled, and Ann found she couldn't stop looking at it.

Her hands began to tremble as an unprecedented sense of unease surged through her. Whether the picture had been meant merely as a prank or as a kind of hidden warning, she didn't know. But for one split second a wash of emotions that were not her own spilled over her—guilt, jealousy, animosity, anger, desperation. All there, all lingering inside the car with her as though whoever had left that picture had also left behind a part of their soul.

With a gasping sob of breath, Ann wadded the picture into a ball and stuffed it deep inside her pocket.

Seven

The sun had gone down, and the light turned to a violet haze that settled like a fine mist over the river. The park was shadowy, lit only by the colorful strings of Japanese lanterns suspended through the trees, and sweetly perfumed by the tangle of wild honeysuckle growing along the steep riverbank. Every once in a while a stray breeze carried the tantalizing aroma from the barbecue grills that were manned by plenty of volunteers.

It was a hot night, made even hotter for Ann by the floodlights trained on the bandstand. For the umpteenth time, she wiped her palms with a tissue she fished from her pocket as she waited for the proceedings to get under way.

Her eyes scanned the crowd, roaming over the familiar faces she had seen that afternoon at the ball park—Jack and Kelly, Donna and Wayne Cooper, Nate Bennett, Mayor Sikes, Viola Pickles—all people she had known most of her life. But because of Drew's proposals, someone out there—

someone she knew—had deliberately left that picture in her car to frighten and intimidate her.

She felt a spurt of anger as the faces swam before her. Riverside Development had pitted friend against friend, neighbor against neighbor. Their promises had ruthlessly exposed the ugly, greedy side of the community—so long marked by the timeless glide of the river, the sweet perfume of flowers, the indolent heat of long, summer days.

That picture had been a graphic reminder to Ann of all that she hated about Riverside Development's plans, and the positive feelings she'd had for Drew that afternoon had all dissolved like a puff of smoke in a windstorm.

Even though she kept her eyes carefully averted, she knew that he was watching her from his side of the tiny stage. Her sensitivity to him was an irritant because try as she might, she couldn't keep her glance from straying in that direction.

He was wearing jeans again tonight, trying to look like one of the boys, Ann thought, her annoyance mounting. Like an ordinary guy.

But ordinary was hardly an adjective that applied. The jeans fit his lean frame like a second skin, and the dark blue polo shirt hugged the muscles of his chest and arms, boldly proclaiming his masculinity.

He caught her eye and smiled, and then he winked, as though they were sharing some intimate secret the rest of the world couldn't know. Without smiling, she turned away.

Mayor Sikes stepped to the podium and gave the microphone a sound thump, which promptly rewarded the crowd with an amplified, ear-splitting scream. The whole front row jumped in unison.

"Let's have a little order here so we can get started. Now, as most of you are aware, the tension in Crossfield lately has been about as thick as my late wife's gravy. I'm mighty ashamed of the way a lot of us—myself included—have been acting since Riverside Development first came to town.

"No one side is completely right or wrong. There's always two ways of looking at a situation. That's why I've asked both Drew Maitland and Ann Lowell to speak with us tonight. Their differing views on Riverside Development will perhaps give each side pause to think about the other, and maybe we can all come up with some sort of compromise. Ann?"

Ann stood, sending the note cards lying in her lap flying. She stooped in dismay to gather them just as Drew leaned down to pick up the ones that had landed at his feet. He handed them to her, his fingers lightly brushing hers. For one brief moment she lingered, unable to break the connection as a current raced from his touch to hers.

Reluctantly she turned away and stepped to the podium, still nervously shuffling through her cards. Toward the back of the crowd, someone let loose with a loud wolf whistle, making Ann's fingers fumble even more.

Finally abandoning her notes, she looked up, letting her gaze once again seek all the familiar faces. And suddenly she knew exactly what to say.

She cleared her throat and bent slightly toward the microphone. Her voice came out clear and strong, and even to her own ears, it held the ring of sincerity. "They say the grass is always greener on the other side of the fence. As you all know, I've been to the other side, and all I can say is that I couldn't wait to get back home."

She paused for a moment, gathering her thoughts. "I lived in the city for eight years, and while I realize Crossfield will never be a city the magnitude of Los Angeles or New York or Dallas, the plans Riverside Development have for our town will alter it drastically and irrevocably."

She spoke more quickly, gaining confidence with her convictions. She talked about the loneliness and isolation of living in a city of strangers and how she'd lived next door to a family for five years without ever having known their names.

She talked about the absence of community and civic pride, and she talked about coming home after having been gone for eight years and being welcomed back with open arms.

She talked about the support she'd been given when she lost her father and her sister, about friends and neighbors and even acquaintances rallying around her for no other reason than to simply be there if she needed them.

She talked about sleeping at night with the river breeze blowing in through open doors and windows, of sitting outside watching the stars, of children playing safely in their own front yards.

She talked about all the things that would be lost and all that would be gained by Riverside Development's plans, but most of all she talked about the need for the community to pull together, not apart, no matter what happened.

When she finished there was dead silence from the crowd, and then the applause thundered in her ears as she took her seat. She saw Donna Cooper smiling and waving at her while her husband, Wayne, flashed her an A-okay sign. A couple of rows back, Bernice Ballard dabbed at her eyes with a lace hanky while Wilma Gates patted her on the back.

Ann felt near tears herself, and the glance she flashed Drew was anything but triumphant. If her words had touched the crowd, they'd also touched her own heart. She'd been completely open and honest about her feelings, and in so doing had revealed a great deal more about herself than she had ever intended.

Drew's blue gaze held hers for a long, soul-searching moment. When he smiled, it was a smile born of pride, a smile that seemed to be telling her, "See? I told you you could do it." Then he rose slowly, and took his place at the podium.

"I won't pretend that's not a hard act to follow," he said with an ironic, thoroughly charming grin. Then he sobered as he scanned the crowd with his piercing blue eyes.

"When I left Crossfield ten years ago, I took a lot of things with me. My love of history and tradition, instilled in me in junior high school by Ms. Viola Pickles. A sense of civic duty and pride in my community that I learned from Mayor Sikes. A keenly developed sense of right and wrong drummed into me at an early age by Sheriff Hayden." He paused for a moment as soft laughter rippled through the crowd.

"I took all that with me and I left nothing behind except a bad reputation. I've come back here after all these years wanting to change that reputation, and wanting to bring something back to the community that had given me so much. I think I can do that with the proposals Riverside Development has set forth."

He spoke then about the renovations along Riverside Drive, about the subdivisions planned for the outlying properties along the river, and the spacious park and community center Riverside planned to donate to the town. He talked on and on about new jobs and opportunities for the youth of Crossfield and Riverside's commitment to the preservation of the community and the beauty of the river. But his last remarks, too, were addressed to the division of the town.

"Riverside Development is deeply committed to this project and to this town. The strength of any community lies within its ability to pull together when the times get hard, to put our own needs aside when a neighbor requires a helping hand. These are trying times, my friends, and we need each other more now than ever. By working together, I know we can reach that compromise Mayor Sikes spoke of."

Once again the applause was loud and long, and Ann saw several people nodding their heads in agreement as they spoke to the person next to them.

Mayor Sikes let the noise die a natural death, then he once again stood at the mike. "This is going to be the shortest speech I've ever made," he told a disbelieving crowd. "Let's eat!"

Several cheers erupted amid much laughter as the assemblage began to break apart and form smaller clusters here and there along the way to the serving tables. As Ann made her way down the platform steps, a circle quickly formed around her as she was complimented and congratulated.

"Your father would have been so proud," Bernice sniffed, patting her hand affectionately.

"You gave us all a lot to think about," Wilma added. "Both you and Drew. Even in opposite corners, you two make quite a team." Her eyes gleamed speculatively as she smiled warmly at Ann.

"Nicely done, Ann," Viola agreed, adjusting the black-rimmed glasses on her nose. "I did think you might have taken a little harder line, though, but all in all it was a very effective speech."

Ann felt Donna, who was standing next to her, poke her in the ribs, and Ann had to work very hard to keep a straight face while Viola added a few more suggestions. Finally Viola left to follow Bernice and Wilma to the barbecue lines, and Ann turned to face Donna.

"Was I really all right?" she asked anxiously.

"You were wonderful," Donna told her sincerely. "There wasn't a dry eye around there toward the end. People who have been at each other's throats for weeks were passing each other tissues."

"I only hope that burst of goodwill lasts," Ann said skeptically, scanning the shadowy grounds for Drew.

She spotted him several feet away, surrounded by his own legion of supporters. Jack and Kelly were among the group around him, and Ann could see Kelly's young face looking up at him, hanging onto his every word, much as she had once done. Ann felt a sharp bite of something she hesitated to put a name to because she hated to be reminded that she was only too capable of feeling jealousy.

"Speaking of goodwill," Donna was saying, "have you and Drew rescheduled your date yet?"

"No." Ann tried to shrug indifferently, but knew it wasn't very convincing. She gave up pretending. "I didn't even know he was back in town until today."

"You mean he didn't call you all week?" Donna asked in disappointment.

"No." Her tone was casual and unconcerned, but Ann couldn't help the niggling little worry that Drew might have someone special in his life in Dallas, someone who made it easy for him to forget about her.

While they stood talking, the band took the stage and struck up their own rendition of 'Satisfaction.' The Stones might have done it better, Ann decided, but certainly not more enthusiastically. She felt herself responding to the music when Jack grabbed her around the waist and pulled her toward the foot of the bandstand, where several couples were already dancing.

"Why aren't you picking on Kelly?" Ann protested, laughing.

"She's not speaking to me," Jack told her casually, holding a beer in one hand while he whirled her around with the other.

"Since when? You two were getting along great earlier."

"Since she saw Drew tonight. You better watch out, cuz. She's liable to give you a run for your money. Or try to." Again Jack spun her, a little more vigorously this time.

Ann stopped. "What do you mean?"

Jack's movements halted, too, as he stared down at her. "I mean Kelly's falling all over him, or haven't you noticed? For some reason, she seems to go for those ambitious, city types."

"That's ridiculous," Ann said with a frown. "Kelly's crazy about you."

"Kelly's crazy about money, which I don't happen to have too much of at the moment."

"You mean since you bought that expensive car," Ann said with a faint note of censure in her tone. "Was that just to impress Kelly?"

Jack smiled but his eyes no longer held the old sparkle. "Maybe it was to impress myself. Hell, it worked for a while," he said with a sudden grin. "Come on, Ann. Cheer up. You always could bring a party down faster than anyone I ever knew."

"Thank you so much," she replied testily.

And then, as if on cue, the band finished the rock and roll number and started up an old love song. As the singer belted out the words to "Crazy," Jack muttered, "Oh, hell," and stomped off into the shadows.

Drew stood talking and laughing with the group of people still clustered around him, but his eyes were trained on the dance floor, where someone had just stepped forward and claimed Ann for the dance. Her long, slender legs—sleekly enhanced by white shorts—moved gracefully in time to the music.

Drew felt himself strangely envious of that man's arms encircling Ann's slender waist, his hands hiding beneath the thick, strands of her glorious hair.

Drew longed to hold her himself, to plunge his fingers into those blazing curls, to kiss her full, sexy lips until they were both breathless. He longed to trace her alluring curves with his hands and feel the satiny warmth of her skin against his. He released a low, frustrated groan that brought a curious glance or two from the persons standing next to him.

The song ended and as everyone moved to the sidelines, the circle around Drew and the one that had surrounded Ann somehow merged. Drew found himself standing directly across from her.

Wayne Cooper playfully patted the top of Ann's head. "Ann looked pretty good up there tonight, didn't she, Drew?"

"Breathtaking."

The conversation around them came to an abrupt halt as Drew realized too late he'd spoken his thoughts aloud, but he decided he didn't much care. The excitement had been building since this afternoon when he had seen her standing at the bottom of the bleachers. He'd freely acknowledged his desire for her then, and she'd answered him, whether she realized it or not. He watched with growing amusement as a slow, apricot stain spread across her cheeks.

The silence stretched for a moment longer before Donna said hastily, "Wayne, why don't you get Ann something to drink. She looks thirsty."

"Yeah, sure." Even Wayne seemed taken aback by the rather obvious undercurrents flowing between Ann and Drew. He returned with several cold beers and handed them all around. Ann took a grateful sip, unsettled by Drew's bold appraisal of her face, especially her mouth.

He was different tonight, she thought nervously. More obvious. More daring. More dangerous.

Somehow he'd maneuvered the small group so that he was standing next to her. His voice was low and intimate as he said in mock surprise, "Angel Lowell drinking beer? I never thought I'd see that. In fact, I don't believe I ever saw you drink anything stronger than a Coke."

"You haven't seen me do a lot of things," Ann assured him coolly.

"You're right about that, but I'm finding that I'd sure like to."

His open aggressiveness in the middle of a crowd shocked her and unnerved her even more. She tried to think of a chilling reply but not one single word came to mind. All she could do was stand there and stare at him, feeling the impact of his blatant sexuality.

What it meant, she didn't know; where it would lead, she didn't dare speculate. But for now, there was no denying that something special was happening between them. Sparks. Electricity. Desire. Whatever it was, Ann's stomach fluttered as if a thousand butterflies had taken up residence.

"Oh, come on, Drew, you've seen Ann drink before," Wayne protested boisterously. "Remember prom night? The spiked punch?"

"Wayne," Donna warned.

"No, really. I remember distinctly. She practically had to be carried out of the place."

"That was Aiden," Ann said quietly.

Drew's gaze clung to hers and something flickered in those blue depths, something that seemed almost a plea. *Don't. Don't let Aiden in on this moment.* Or had that silent appeal sprang from her own mind?

"Take your foot out of your mouth, Wayne, so you can dance with me," Donna scolded as she pulled her husband, rather roughly, toward the other dancers.

The haunting strands of "Only You" floated softly through the park, wrapping around Ann's senses like a lover's caress. Like Drew's caress, she thought with a strange ache deep inside her.

Jack and Kelly were already dancing, obviously having made up, as their bodies pressed tightly together and they barely swayed to the slow, sensuous beat. Their movements, though slight, were brazenly suggestive, leaving no room to speculate how their evening would end. Watching them, Ann became even more acutely aware of the man standing next to her.

Across the river the first set of fireworks shot high into the sky, clustering into red and blue and white sparks as they exploded with a boom. The crowd oohed and aahed as they began moving toward the bank. Ann started forward with them, but Drew caught her arm.

"I know where there's a better view." Not waiting for her refusal, he led her away from the crowd and through a thick stand of trees, where the riverbanks rose to a steep bluff on either side. They stood above the crowd, alone, as the night sky came alive with dazzling light.

From their vantage it seemed that the splashes of fire and color were directly above them, enveloping them in breath-taking brilliance, showering them with drops of light. Drew stood behind her, not touching her and yet touching her in a way that was frighteningly sensuous. Then his arms slipped around her waist, holding her close, and Ann let him, because just for a moment, they were lost and alone in a glorious universe.

And all too quickly it came to an end.

The sound of thunder died away with one last echo, the night sky calmed and darkened. But Drew did not take away his arms. He tightened them, in fact, pulling her against him as he buried his face in her hair.

She resisted, tried to pull away, but he held her. "Time to pay up, Angel," he whispered into her ear.

Anticipation tightened the breath in her throat. "Wh-what are you talking about?"

"After the game today. You wanted me to kiss you then, didn't you? I could see it in your eyes."

"No! How dare you—"

"Yes, I dare," he murmured, parting her hair and pressing his lips against the back of her neck. "I've dared to admit what you keep trying to deny."

"I don't know what you're talking about," she said breathlessly, tipping her head slightly forward as his lips slid along her nape.

"Then let me spell it out for you." His voice thrummed in her ear, sending hot shivers along her skin. "I still want you. Just as much as I ever did. Maybe more."

He turned her in his arms, and her eyes were drawn immediately to his. In the bold moonlight she could see his face clearly and the heat in his blue gaze stopped her heart. The whole world stopped, and then started again, in slow motion this time, each passing moment excruciatingly prolonged and intense. But Ann did not move away.

He lowered his head, and his mouth touched hers, tenderly, cautiously. Ann's lips trembled beneath his. He pulled back for a moment, looking deeply into her eyes, and she returned his stare, trapped by what she saw. All of the lost years, all the loneliness and pain and longing, all of her unshed tears were there in Drew's eyes. But it was only a glance, a very brief impression, because in an instant his mouth locked onto hers once more in an almost desperate hunger.

His mouth devoured hers as his hands glided over her back to her waist, down to her hips. His tongue begged, persuaded, demanded, until Ann responded willingly, opening her mouth to him. His lips seared hers, made the butterflies go wild inside her stomach, and set her nice, safe little world into a blazing inferno.

He tore his mouth from hers, burying his hands in her hair as he tilted her face to his. "It's still there. Do you feel it?" he demanded in a low, ragged voice.

"Yes," she whispered, and then she breathed his name against his lips just before he took her mouth again in deep, probing thrusts that grew more urgent with each pounding heartbeat.

His mouth was so hot, the air so still and thick and close. Ann clung to him, pressing against his hardness as her world spun and raced with mindless, melting pleasure. She was falling, but Drew's arms were around her, catching her, steadying her, and then driving her to desperation.

Their mouths still fused, his hands stroked against her thighs and hips, along her waist and ribs, then down again to tug loose the hem of her shirt from her shorts. His fingers stole along her naked flesh, teasing, then pausing briefly when he met with no barrier. With a deep, sensuous groan, he slid his hand around to cover her bare breast.

Lifting his mouth from hers, he traced her jawline with his lips, pausing to whisper deep, dark promises that left her hot and quivering with a long-hidden need. He pulled her shirt upward, exposing her breasts, and bending suddenly, his mouth replaced his hand. Ann's head fell back, her eyes tightly closed.

She'd never experienced passion before, she realized weakly. Certainly not with David, not even with Drew years ago. Not like this. Everything, *everything* was obliterated but the feel of his lips against her breast, the sound of his low whispers in the dark, the feel of his hand, burning against her skin.

The tiny tremors shooting through her, faster and faster, brought Ann fully alert as she realized what was about to happen. And then she became aware of something else, a sound. Voices.

"Drew, Drew, stop!" She tried to push him away as she struggled against him.

Slowly he lifted his head, staring down at her in confusion. "Honey, what's wrong?"

"Someone's coming," she whispered furiously.

Drew's head snapped around at the approaching voices through the trees. They automatically stepped apart, and Drew moved in front of Ann while she hastily adjusted her clothing.

"Drew, is that you?" Jack called as he and Kelly detached themselves from the shadows and moved toward Ann and Drew. "What the devil are you doing out here in the dark—" His voice broke off abruptly as he noticed Ann standing behind Drew.

"We came out here to enjoy the fireworks," Drew said matter-of-factly. His voice betrayed nothing of the intense emotion that had just passed between them, but Ann's face still flamed, her hands still trembled, her body still quivered. She was certain that she would never be the same.

"Looks like the show's over," Jack muttered, and Kelly laughed softly into the darkness.

Ann's face grew even hotter, but Drew merely said, "Doesn't it? In that case, I guess we'll head back."

Ann lifted her chin and sailed past all of them with only a muttered "Good night." She left dead silence in her wake. She could feel their stares on her retreating back, knew that they had read the situation correctly. And it didn't help any when Drew caught up with her and placed a possessive arm over her shoulder as they walked back toward the park. If Jack and Kelly had had any doubts before about what they'd interrupted, they certainly wouldn't now, Ann thought with a sudden wave of bitterness.

"Do you have to advertise?" she said angrily, shrugging Drew's arm off her shoulder as they neared the park.

"Why not? I'm not ashamed of what we were doing. It was perfectly natural."

"There was nothing perfect or natural about it," Ann snapped. "It was a huge mistake." They had stopped in the shadows near the edge of the park, and she took a few steps away, distancing herself from him. Instead of knocking down barriers, what had almost happened a few moments earlier had erected new ones. Ann was embarrassed and furious with herself for her lack of control. And she was furious with Drew for still having a hold over her.

She knew he was staring at her, but she couldn't see his expression in the darkness. "Why is it a mistake," he asked slowly, "that we still have feelings for each other? We're both free now."

"Free?" She gave a low, bitter laugh. "We'll never be free. There're too many things between us. And the feelings we have for each other are all the wrong ones."

He took a step toward her. "What do you mean?"

"The love, the trust, the sharing—they're all gone, Drew. What we feel for each other now is purely physical. It's...chemistry or something," she said crisply, crossing her arms in front of her. "Don't you see? It's what's gone that matters. We don't even know each other anymore. Maybe the attraction is still there, but it isn't enough."

"Why not? Isn't that the way most relationships start? With physical attraction?"

She stared at him for a moment, startled. "I don't want a relationship with you. I don't want anything from you."

He was standing in front of her now, staring down at her. His face was still shadowed but Ann had no trouble reading the stubborn set of his jaw, the rigid line of his mouth. "How do you know that?" he persisted. "Didn't you just say we don't know each other anymore? I want to see you again, Ann. Tomorrow night."

"I don't think so."

"You were ready to have dinner with me the other night, before Donna had to go to the hospital." His tone altered slightly. "Or was my first assumption correct? Was that just an excuse so you wouldn't have to see me?"

"Of course not," Ann denied quickly, perhaps a shade too quickly, she worried. "But if you were as eager to see me as you let on..." She let her words trail off in confusion.

"What?"

She hesitated for a moment, then said in a rush, "You didn't even call me when you got back to town. I didn't even know you were back until I saw you at the game today. It just seems to me that I'm awfully easy for you to forget, Drew. You did for ten years."

His eyes, deep and intense, held her gaze. Even in the darkness, she found she couldn't look away.

"Not one day has gone by in all those years that I haven't thought about you."

"Then why did you wait so long to come back?" Ann asked desperately. "I've asked myself that question so many times, and the only answer I can think of is that—" She bit her lip as her voice began to tremble. "I have to wonder, Drew, if it's me you really want."

He glared down at her as though she were crazy. "What the hell's that supposed to mean?"

Her arms were still folded in front of her. She tightened them around herself. "When you look at me, is it me you see? Or is it . . . Aiden?"

He said nothing, merely continued to stare at her. Then he grabbed her shoulders, his fingers biting into her flesh. "Don't you understand anything? It was always you I saw. How do you think I ever stood touching her? Because she had *your* face. I never loved her."

Ann closed her eyes for a moment, trying to repair her defenses against the words that she had longed to hear for too many years. "How can I believe that when you were with her for so long, even after she lost the baby? And after the divorce you never came back." The words *to me* were left unspoken, but they clung to the charged air around them like the remnants of a bad dream.

Drew paused, wondering if he should tell her all of it, including Aiden's final ultimatum, the one that had all but destroyed him. He saw the slight quiver of her mouth, could feel her trembling beneath his hands. She was close to crumbling and he wasn't sure if he dared go on, if his purpose would be served by cutting her that deeply.

In the end what he finally said was, "I didn't think I had the right to come to you. Not after what I'd done. It's taken all these years for me to put that part of my life behind me. We're two different people now, Ann. Can't we forget the past and move forward?"

"There is no forward for you and me. It's over."

"It is *not* over." He slid his hands slowly down her arms, then gently tugged loose her grasp. "Did it feel like it was over a few minutes ago?" he asked softly. His hands moved back up her arms, feathering over her shoulders. "It felt more like the beginning to me." One hand moved to the back of her neck, gently urging her toward him.

"You're not being fair," Ann said, her arms dropping to her sides.

"I'm tired of being fair," Drew said roughly. "Just tell me one thing." His arms captured her again, pulling her against him, holding her close in spite of her resistance. "Do you still care, Angel? Or is it my imagination, my wishful thinking?"

Her sigh fell softly into the darkness. "I... don't know. No, I don't... I can't."

"Because of Aiden?" There was deep pain and a trace of resignation in his voice, but he said with stubborn resolve, "We've both made our reparations. We did the right thing for too many years. It's our turn now."

Ann felt the truth of his words hit her like the aftermath of an earthquake. The burden of guilt, so long resting on her shoulders, seemed to lift and float away. She could almost believe what he said was true.

"It isn't over, Ann," he whispered against her ear.

Ann shivered in response, her eyes fluttering closed. "I'm beginning to realize that," she said breathlessly. "But, Drew, I can't make you any promises."

His voice was low and soft and infinitely seductive as he murmured against her lips, "I think you just did."

Ann came abruptly awake with the uneasy notion that a noise had disturbed her sleep. She sat up in bed, eyes staring wide into the darkness. Turning on the bedside lamp, she anxiously searched the room with her gaze.

Sometime during the night the wind had picked up. She could hear the rustle of leaves outside her bedroom window. The gauzy curtains whipped and twisted in the breeze, the ends snaking across the polished surface of her dresser. On the floor in front of the dresser, a picture frame lay face down, a victim of the wind.

Ann got out of bed and crossed the room, stooping to pick up the picture. She cried out in dismay as a jagged piece of glass sliced the end of her finger. The frame slipped from her hand and fell to the floor, right side up this time. Holding her finger tightly, Ann stared down at the photogragh of her and Aiden. She shivered suddenly as a cold draft of wind crawled across her skin.

A jagged crack in the glass split the image in two, severing Ann from her sister. A drop of her own blood was smeared across the glass covering her heart.

She wasn't sure why—perhaps because of the picture she'd found earlier that day in her car; perhaps because it was the dead of night—but that ruined photograph seemed portentous somehow. An omen of something she did not yet understand.

Eight

As Drew wheeled into a parking space in front of the Crossfield Motel, he realized he was probably going to be late for the only date that had mattered to him in over ten years. Cutting off the engine, he flashed a quick glance at his wristwatch, hoping to find a discrepancy with the clock on the dash. No such luck.

With a silent oath, he jerked open the car door, yanked out his briefcase and hurried up the metal steps to his second-floor room, cursing Mayor Sikes for his long-windedness, which was about as effective as cursing rain in April or the heat in July. All of them were inevitable.

He'd spent the entire afternoon with the mayor and several ladies from the Historical Society walking Riverside Drive, mapping out his proposals for renovations, drawing sketches for their inspection and answering endless questions, many of them having absolutely nothing to do with Riverside Development.

Wilma Gates and Bernice Ballard had seemed particularly interested to find out how he was making out with Ann—concerning the sale of her land, Bernice had quickly added, then nudged Wilma knowingly when she thought he wasn't looking. The council vote for rezoning was coming up, they reminded him. Had Ann changed her mind about that? Did he know about Adam Lowell's will, the trust funds, the deathbed promise Ann had made to her father?

Hell, they knew more about Ann's business than he did, and Drew wasn't above asking a few questions of his own. He hoped his had been a little more subtle, but looking back now, he doubted he'd fooled anyone.

Unlocking the door, he tossed his briefcase onto the bed and headed straight for the bathroom, hopping on first one foot then the other as he pulled off his shoes and heaved them toward the closet.

Quickly undressing, he climbed into the shower, knowing it would do no good to wait for the water to warm. A hot shower was only a memory at the Crossfield Motel. Shivering and muttering graphic suggestions to the management, he let the cold stream of water pelt his skin.

With brisk, efficient movements, he lathered his hair and soaped his body as he tried to analyze the source of his aggravation. He was nervous and edgy, and it had nothing to do with the cold water or the council vote or anything else concerning his job. He was worried about tonight, about how things would progress with Angel. *If* they would progress at all.

Patience, he reminded himself grimly. He'd had ten long years to learn that. He and Angel were starting over. Once more their lives had joined, and this time he had to make it right. This time he couldn't afford any mistakes. He was too much of a pragmatist to believe in fate or destiny, but he did believe he and Angel were meant to be together.

Now, he just had to convince her of the same thing.

* * *

Why had she agreed to go out with him? Ann asked herself for the hundredth time as she pulled her car onto the highway and headed toward town. She couldn't remember being this nervous for a date since—actually, since the first time she'd gone out with Drew back in high school.

It had seemed silly even back then to be so agitated. She and Drew had been friends for a long time. When he'd finally asked her out, it should have seemed the most natural thing in the world, but Ann had been in a frenzy all day, fussing over her clothes, worrying about what she would say and how she would act, anxiously wondering whether he'd find her attractive.

Not unlike tonight, she decided, and that thought gave her very little comfort. She found her behavior annoying, in fact. *For heaven's sake, you're a grown woman,* she admonished herself. *And Drew Maitland is just a man, and this is just a dinner date.*

Wrong on both counts. Drew Maitland was not just any man and there was no use pretending otherwise; he was the man she had once loved more than anything or anyone and he was the man who had torn her life apart. And tonight wasn't just a dinner date; it was a night of reckoning, a night for some hard decisions on both their parts, a night she wasn't at all sure she was ready to face.

Ann rolled down her window and let the rush of wind sweep across her skin as it lifted the heavy red curls from her neck. The night was beautiful, warm and clear with a blanket of stars covering the sky and a waxing moon staring pale among the dark silhouette of the woods. The fence rows along the side of the road were tangled with honeysuckle vines that perfumed the air with a lovely, sweet fragrance. It was a night, like so many summer nights long ago.

Ann's hands clenched tightly on the steering wheel, her knuckles whitening as she sped along the highway, toward town, toward Drew. She wouldn't do this, she resolved. She would not let herself be caught up in memories and emotions that belonged in the past. The momentary softness she'd yielded to fled. Her mouth hardened once again.

Seeing Drew, letting him back into her life was leaving herself wide open for the kind of devastation that had taken her so long to get over. She had built up her defenses over the years, she had guarded herself well...until now. But she had not reckoned on Drew's return, nor the powerful hold he still had over her. She had learned in a frighteningly short space of time that her fragile shields were no match for him.

The restaurant Ann had chosen was one of the new ones that had seemingly sprung up overnight to accommodate Crossfield's sudden prosperity. Located near the river on the outskirts of town, the Riverboat Landing was a trendy dining place for the newcomers in the area. Most of the natives still frequented the establishments in town, and that was the main reason Ann had made the selection. She hoped that she and Drew would not run into anyone they knew. She'd had a hard enough time explaining tonight to herself, much less to anyone else.

Pulling into a darkened, secluded corner of the parking lot, Ann got out of the car and crossed the pavement to the restaurant, smoothing the wrinkles from her dress as she walked. Of all the outfits she'd sifted through, she wondered now why she'd chosen this particular one—an off-the-shoulder dress in clinging black knit with a mid-thigh hemline. In L.A. the dress wouldn't have gotten a second glance; in Crossfield, it suddenly seemed a bit too daring and flashy, a dress more suited to Aiden than to her.

But not anymore, Ann reminded herself firmly, squaring her shoulders in determination. She'd changed in the last ten years. She'd had to. She was no longer the clinging, insecure young woman Drew had betrayed, a woman whose confidence in her own attractiveness had been all but destroyed for a long, long time. She wasn't Angel anymore.

She'd dressed this way because she had something to prove, not just to Drew, but to herself.

He was sitting at the bar when she entered through the stained-glass door of the restaurant. She could see his reflection in the ornate mirror behind the bar, and she stood for a moment, letting her gaze roam over his features, taking in at once the strong line of jaw and chin, the bold slash of his brows above eyes that were the most magnetic blue she had ever seen. His hair, glistening gold highlights under the artificial lighting, looked slightly damp, as though he'd just stepped from the shower. A tantalizing thought in its own right, Ann mused as she let her gaze drop to the broad shoulders beneath the expensive-looking sport coat. His hands, large and strong and well-formed, were resting on the bar on either side of an untouched drink.

Ann lifted her eyes and their gazes collided in the mirror. She felt heat touch her cheeks as she wondered how long he'd been watching her watching him.

The barest knowing smile touched his lips, telling her he'd seen enough and he'd enjoyed every minute of it.

Her blush deepened as she realized his answering appraisal was just as thorough as hers had been. His smoldering scrutiny started her heart pounding with an almost painful awareness. She took a long breath and let it out, putting on a determinedly casual face as she started toward him, her heels echoing hollowly on the wooden planks of the floor.

Drew turned from the bar and stood as he watched her approach.

"Sorry I'm late," she apologized with a stiff, little smile.

"No problem. It was well worth the wait," he said appreciatively as his gaze flicked over her once more.

He bent suddenly, letting his lips brush across her cheek, and Ann's synthetic poise faded. He smelled of soap and some undeniably masculine cologne. She felt her heart go into double time as she slid onto the bar stool next to him and crossed her black-stockinged legs, an action that did not go unnoticed or, judging by the subtle gleam in the depths of those blue eyes, unappreciated by Drew. She saw his gaze slide up and down her legs before he once again met her eyes.

"Nice dress."

"Thank you," she said primly, trying to mask the unfamiliar warmth stealing over her. Their sexual attraction was almost a tangible thing, an electrical current that sizzled and crackled between them. She turned her own gaze toward the bartender and gave him her drink order. The glass of white wine was promptly set before her, and Ann took a nervous sip, ever aware of Drew's steady inspection.

"Why do you keep staring at me?" she finally blurted in annoyance. "You're making me nervous."

He laughed softly, forcing her gaze to mingle with his. "I guess I just can't get over the changes in you—the way you look, the way you dress... and act." He smiled ironically, staring pointedly at the wineglass in her hand. "Beer last night, wine tonight. I can't believe this is the same woman who used to lecture me on the evils of alcohol."

Ann grimaced, wrinkling her nose in distaste. "Don't remind me. I suppose I did tend to be a bit self-righteous in those days. But I hope I've matured a little since then. Not that I think drinking is a sign of maturity," she added dryly.

Drew smiled. "And I've learned that moderation, in a lot of things, can be a virtue. I guess we've both changed. But you're just as beautiful as ever, and you still have the sexiest legs in Texas."

His voice had taken on a sort of lazy, intimate drawl that sent a warning shiver scurrying down her spine. Ann laughed self-consciously, knowing full well that she certainly did not have the sexiest legs in Texas. But she was flattered by the outrageous compliment anyway, and not a little flustered. "Well, that certainly covers a lot of territory," she tried to reply lightly.

Drew's blue eyes sparkled wickedly. "Which is more than I can say for that dress."

"Drew!" she admonished in a husky voice she barely recognized as her own. How had this happened? she wondered suddenly. How had she come to be sitting here, casually flirting with a man who had once destroyed her life? She was actually enjoying herself, enjoying the anticipation of the evening as though it might—*could*—lead to something.

Their eyes met for a moment and held, and Ann knew instinctively that the same thought had occurred to Drew. And then his name was called, and the moment swirled away, leaving Ann with an odd feeling of loss as she rose and followed the hostess to their table set in a cozy window alcove overlooking the river.

A candle flashed and flickered in its fat jar as she and Drew were seated and handed menus. Ann studied the selections for far longer than was necessary, but for some reason, she found herself unable to meet Drew's gaze, reluctant to face what had just passed between them.

"Have you had any more trouble with trespassers?" Drew asked, sipping his drink after they'd placed their dinner orders and the waitress had disappeared.

"No, not since the day you were there. Whoever it was probably realized how close he'd come to hitting someone and got scared. At least, I hope so."

"Did you talk to Sheriff Hayden?" Drew persisted softly.

"I didn't really see the point," Ann said with a careless shrug. "There was nothing he could do, and besides, I... forgot."

Because Drew had been on her mind the rest of the day, Ann remembered, feeling herself blush slightly. "I'll mention it to him the next time I see him," she said dismissively, clasping her hands in her lap. The picture of the burning angel came instantly to her mind, but Ann didn't want to tell Drew about that. Talking about it seemed to attach more significance than was warranted, and the incident had already begun to fade from her mind. Besides, nothing else had happened. Better just to forget about it all together, she decided.

"Let's talk about something else," she suggested quickly.

"All right. So tell me what you've been doing for the last ten years."

Ann looked up in surprise. How strange that he should ask that, she thought, as though this was the first time they had seen each other in years. And maybe it was. Maybe up until this point, they hadn't really seen each other at all.

She studied his shadowed features in the dancing candlelight. She could see the mirrored flicker of the flame in the blue depths of his eyes—or was that another kind of fire?

She shivered slightly, letting her gaze drop as she answered automatically. "Years and years of school. Teaching. Writing. Not much to tell actually."

"I don't believe that for a minute. Tell me about your work," he pressed gently. "Do you enjoy teaching?"

She rested her elbows on the table and let her hands cup her chin. "Yes, I do. I love history, I love books, and I like sharing that love with my students. Academia is a whole different world, you know. You can lose yourself in it. I guess that's what I wanted to do in a way."

"Did I make you want to hide?"

She felt his eyes on her, compelling, intense, drawing her own gaze. She lifted one slender shoulder. "It wasn't just you. I had a hard time facing a lot of things back then." She smiled wistfully. "Anyway, after so many years in school, the campus had become my home. It seemed perfectly natural to stay."

There was a subtle pause as Drew continued to regard her in the soft, wavering light. "Is that where you met him?"

There was no mistaking who he meant, and Ann didn't try to pretend otherwise. "Yes. We had a math class together my first semester at U.C.L.A. I needed help, and he volunteered."

"I'll bet he did."

At his tone, Ann's brows drew together in a frown. "That was a long time ago."

"It was only a moment ago for me."

The simplicity of his words stunned her, shattered what little pretense might have remained between them. The deep pain in his eyes caused her own to moisten, her throat to tighten, and she was reminded anew just what the last ten years had cost them both. She turned her gaze toward the silent, timeless glide of the river as she felt his hand close over hers on the table.

"Have you been happy all this time?"

Had she been happy? She had a home, a successful fulfilling career, lots of friends. She had done very well for herself, had made a good life, and she had done it without Drew. But had she been happy?

Her sigh came from deep within her soul as she looked into those dark, searching eyes. "I don't find myself thinking about happiness too much anymore. Do you?"

"No, I guess I don't." For the longest time he stared at her, the blue of his eyes intense. "But I'm happy tonight, being here with you," he added softly, gripping her hand tightly for a moment before releasing it.

His words touched her in a way she could not name. For just a whisper of a moment, they had shared a glimpse into each other's souls and seen the loneliness there, the vulnerability. And even when the curtain had once again fallen, Ann had the strangest feeling that she had just found her way home after having been lost for a long time.

Then the realization hit her that she had missed *him,* missed his quick understanding and his deep friendship, just as surely as she had missed his love.

The waitress brought their dinners and they concentrated on eating, the slight attempts at conversation were kept light and impersonal. But after the plates had been taken away, Ann couldn't even remember what she had eaten. Her mind was too distracted, too drawn to the magnetic, virile man across from her.

"Dessert?" he inquired in a teasing, almost affectionate tone. "As I recall, you used to have an insatiable sweet tooth."

Ann shook her head. "Not anymore. Like you, I've learned the virtue of moderation."

One brow lifted ruefully. "Yet another change. I wonder if there are others," he said softly, letting his gaze wander carelessly over her face, then dropping and lingering on the bare skin at her shoulders. Suddenly the teasing light in his eyes was replaced by a dark, raw passion that burned into her skin as thoroughly as if he had touched her with an ember.

"We...haven't even discussed the Riverside project," Ann stammered, unsettled by the intensity of his regard. "Wasn't that the purpose of this dinner?"

"You mean it's time for me to start convincing you?" he asked in a low, husky voice that she had no trouble at all deciphering.

Her green eyes were wide and guileless as she stared back at him. "Well...yes...I guess so."

He rested his forearms on the table and leaned toward her. "All right, how's this? You know what I'd like to do right now? I'd like to go down to the river, strip off all our clothes and go swimming like we used to on hot nights. I remember one night in particular...." He let his voice trail off, then added softly, "You're remembering it, too, aren't you?"

How could she help it? That memory was always with her. If she closed her eyes, she could almost feel the cool water lapping against her skin, a fine counterpoint to the warmth of Drew's body when he had held her close.

She had always imagined that when they finally made love, it would be there, in their special place where they had shared their dreams. It had almost happened there one night, when they'd both lost control, when Drew's kisses had taken her beyond the point of thinking, when his caresses had had her clinging to him instead of pushing him away. Every facet of that night had been solidly imbedded in her memory—the feel of his lips on her breasts, the touch of his hands as he sought her most sensitive places....

Ann shivered, feeling a sudden thrill at the base of her spine. The image of that night had teased and tormented her for so many years. She'd often wondered, especially during the bad times, if she hadn't stopped them that night, how their lives might have been changed. If they had made love then, perhaps Drew wouldn't have turned to Aiden.

"I've dreamed about that night," he continued, so accurately tracking her own thoughts. "I remember every single detail, how cool the water felt gliding against our skin, how smooth and hot your body felt beneath my hands. I remember our whispers in the darkness and how beautiful you looked with only the moonlight covering you."

Ann closed her eyes, his voice washing over her like a heated wave. In the midst of a noisy crowd, without so much as a single touch, he was slowly, thoroughly, seducing her. The voices in the background faded; their surroundings vanished. They were back on the bank of that moonlit river, alone, two lost souls needing each other.

Ann opened her eyes and let her gaze link with his once more. His eyes were deep and dark, inviting her to explore the secret growing between them.

"It should have happened that night, Angel," he murmured, his voice low and liquid with persuasion. "It could happen tonight. I want to make love to you, and I think you want it, too."

Desire, hot and glowing and ready to erupt flowed between them. But what then? Ann wondered. What else was there between them anymore? Love? After ten years? She doubted it. What if they found out after all the elapsed time that there was nothing between them but a lot of wasted years. She had lived with this *longing* for so long she wasn't sure how she'd feel if it were no longer there. Relief? Strangely enough, she didn't think so.

His gaze, deep and searching, clung to hers, as if trying to recapture the moment, the memory, the intimate mood they had shared. But it was too late. Ann deliberately sealed off her emotions, and in so doing, found she could not quite meet his eyes anymore.

They both rose and Ann led the way out of the restaurant and across the parking lot to her car. The pale drift of mist from the river softened the night. A stray current of air rustled through the leaves of the water oaks and the air smelled heavy with flowers and the scent of the coming rain. Ann leaned against her car door as Drew propped one arm on the roof and stood staring down at her.

"What happened in there?" he inquired mildly.

"I don't know what you mean."

"You used to be completely honest with yourself and with me. Has that changed, as well?" he asked with a faint note of censure.

At his accusation, Ann felt a flicker of anger that died almost instantly. He was right, after all. She could evade, pretend, even lie as much as she wanted to, but eventually she would have to face the truth. She just wasn't sure she was ready to.

She pushed her hair back over her shoulder with an impatient hand. "I think we should take things slowly, Drew. We don't even know each other anymore."

"We can get to know each other again. In fact, I'd like that very much," he added with a devastating smile. "I find myself completely intrigued by this new woman, and I'm dying to know if there's anything remaining of the old one."

Without even being aware of it, he'd touched on part of the problem. She folded her arms defensively over her breasts. "Would you be disappointed if there were?"

"Absolutely not. As fascinating as this new woman is, I still remember the old one being irresistible in her own right." He paused for a moment, then added in a low, completely determined voice, "I want to spend time with you, Ann."

Ann gazed into the swirling mist at her feet as if searching for answers there instead of in her heart. "So much is happening," she said at last. "Not just to us, but around us. All the animosity in town, the council vote..." She let her voice trail off as she shrugged helplessly.

"Is that all it is?" Warm, purposeful hands smoothed over her shoulders and down her arms, pulling her into his embrace. "Tell me the truth," he demanded, his deep voice whispering through her soul.

Ann felt the sigh that gathered in her lungs as she rested her head against the hard wall of his chest. Beneath her ear, his heart beat a strong, reassuring cadence. "Wanting you frightens me," she admitted bleakly. "You make me too aware of feelings I've tried for a long time to deny."

There was a long pause, then, "Are you afraid I'll hurt you again?"

She leaned back in his arms and gazed up at him, her defenses down, her heart revealed in her eyes. "That's part of it. I know it sounds strange, but in a way, I think I'm just as frightened that you won't. Or that you can't. It scares me to think that after all we've been through, there might be nothing left, that it might all turn out to be one huge disappointment."

He smiled down at her. "You mean the game can't possibly live up to the buildup?"

She was amazed again by his intuition. She smiled, too. "Something like that."

"Wouldn't it be better if we found that out rather than go on wondering?" He pulled her back into his arms, letting his fingers play through the thick strands of her hair. When he spoke again, his voice had deepened, become more sensual, sending a wave of heat rippling through Ann's body. "I want you, more than I've ever wanted anyone. But I can't make you any promises on how either of us will or won't feel afterward."

She pulled back in protest, but he stilled her movement by tightening his arms around her. "We're being honest here and that's just the way it is. That's the way life is. We both know that. But I can promise you one thing—" he paused, his lips curving in a secret, seductive smile as he stared down at her "—I'll do everything in my power *not* to disappoint you."

She felt his hands glide over her rib cage and brush against the sides of her breasts as he bent his head, his breath tingling sensuously along her skin.

"Ann." His voice was a husky murmur in her ear.

Silence. Ann's nerves screamed with alertness as her heart began to thud in slow, painful strokes. Instinctively she turned her head just enough to meet his waiting lips, surrendering fully to their pressure. A shudder passed from his body to hers as the passion pulsed between them, stripping them both of caution. Their tongues met and mingled and the kiss intensified with a hot, hungry insistence. His heartbeat pounded against her breast as her hands slid beneath his jacket and around him, savoring the feel of his hard-muscled flesh beneath the soft texture of his shirt.

With a low, masculine groan, Drew tore his mouth from hers, pulled her even more tightly into his embrace. "The magic is still there, Angel," he whispered reverently. "How could we be disappointed?"

Ann let her head fall back in a silent, sensuous response to his words, her lips parted and waiting.

He touched her mouth with teasing kisses, then slowly slid his lips across her cheek, lingering at her ear for a moment before burying his face in the hollow of her neck. Ann locked her hands behind his neck, feeling the soft, gold-streaked hair beneath her fingers.

At last Drew pulled back, but only to whisper hoarsely, "Oh, sweetheart." He cradled her head against his shoulder, resting his cheek against her hair. They stood that way for a long moment, neither of them speaking, as their hearts pounded against one another's. "Come back to my room with me," he urged softly. "I need you so much."

How easy it would be to go with him, to surrender fully to a passion that had been simmering for so many years. How easy it would be to forget, for one beautiful moment, that it couldn't last, that it would never be just the two of them.

Oh, but to have again, even for a moment, what she had waited for, wished for. *Be careful what you wish for.*

And with that thought, the moment slid away, swallowed up by the dark mists of their past.

"Drew, please try to understand. I'm just not ready for this."

He pushed the fiery curls over her shoulders, letting one hand remain to caress the tender skin at her neck. "Believe it or not, I do understand. But I'd like for you to try to understand my feelings, as well. Seeing you again, being with you, remembering everything we had—I can't stand back and do nothing. Not now, not when there's nothing standing in our way."

"There's more to consider than just you and me," Ann reminded him darkly. "The whole town is depending on both of us. I can't forget my obligations. I can't let you *make* me forget them."

Abruptly his arms dropped from around her and he turned away, shoving his fingers through his hair in frustration. "You're right of course. There always are obligations, obstacles, excuses."

"Drew—" She put a tentative hand to his sleeve. "I can't help how I feel. It's just that the time is not right."

He turned back to her, the lines of bitterness cut deeply into his face. "I'm beginning to wonder if the time will ever be right for us."

Nine

It was too hot to sleep. The sluggish rotation of the ceiling fan barely stirred the warm, sticky air. Ann moved restlessly in bed, kicking off the clinging sheet as she willed herself to sleep. But it wasn't the heat that kept her from resting.

She was haunted tonight. Haunted by her thoughts and her memories of Drew, haunted by the way he had held her earlier, the way he had kissed her and the way she had responded. She was haunted by the awareness that Drew's smoldering desire was matched by her own. And she was haunted by the remaining guilt of wanting a man who should never have been in her thoughts.

But, dear God, she did want him, had wanted him for so very long. Wanted him even when she'd had no knowledge of what the deep ache inside her meant. Wanted him even after he had betrayed her, when her love had turned to hate. Wanted him even when he had been her sister's husband.

For ten years she had yearned for him, burned for his touch during long, sleepness nights.

Like tonight.

With an impatient sigh, Ann swung her legs off the bed and strode across the room to the open window. A breeze blew through the room, rustling the curtains, fanning the moist curls framing her face. She closed her eyes, lifting her hair, letting the wind sweep across her neck. She could smell the honeysuckle outside her window. The thick, sweet scent only added to her restlessness.

Her eyes fastened on a light, minute and far away, in the house that had once belonged to the Maitlands. Once upon a time that light would have been a signal for her to meet Drew down by the river. His light would have remained on until midnight, waiting for her responding sign.

Ann glanced at her watch. Midnight had come and gone.

From the spot where he stood near the old river bridge, Drew could pinpoint Ann's bedroom window in the farmhouse. He'd watched the light in her room for a long time, even caught a glimpse of her silhouette once or twice, before the light had gone out and he'd forced his attention back to the river.

The night was hot, hot and humid and heavy with the threat of rain. The air crackled with tension, waiting... waiting...

It was the heat, he'd told himself, that had driven him from his bed at the Crossfield Motel. The heat that had brought him unerringly to the river. The heat and a restless urgency that had kept him discontent for over a decade.

A warm breeze filtered through the willows, stirring the long branches that dipped and trailed in the water. And with the wind came the undeniable scent of honeysuckle, unbearably sweet, haunting, like a dream that had never quite finished.

"Angel." He whispered her name in the hot, waiting stillness, wondering if she was sleeping, and if not, was she as restless as he was tonight? Was she thinking about the feel of their bodies coming together earlier, their mouths joining? Thinking about her now, Drew could feel his body tightening as desire stabbed through him.

And she wanted him, too. He could read it in her beautiful, bewitching eyes. But she'd said the love was gone, the warmth and tenderness they'd once shared were only memories. Maybe she was right. Maybe they couldn't recapture what they'd had. But there was still so much between them, so many feelings he couldn't deny.

"You're wrong, Angel," he said softly, his words echoing across the dark, mirrored water. "The time has never been more right."

The river path was softly lit by the pale, sterling moon, but the stars that had shone so brilliantly earlier were now veiled by clouds. Buttercups and primrose edged against the path and in places thick, silver-green moss had completely overrun it, making it seem neglected and forgotten. In the distance an owl called once, restless and forlorn in the deepening shadows of the woods. It was a call that matched Ann's mood.

Loneliness was nothing new to her. She couldn't remember a time in the the last ten years—even in a crowd—when she hadn't felt lonely. She'd learned to deal with it, live with it, sometimes to even be comforted by it. But tonight...

Tonight she remembered only too well the reason for the loneliness, the longing, the dreams that were always left unfinished. She remembered why happiness was a hazy memory from the distant past.

She could smell the river now, could hear the soft liquid sounds as the water lapped at the banks. She stood for a moment on the high bank, staring down at the shimmering ribbon of water. Then she found the stone steps set into the side of the bluff and climbed down to the tiny, grassy beach that had once been her trysting place with Drew.

The breeze skimming the water carried a hint of moisture. Dropping her towel to the ground, she bent to remove her sandals, then sat down on the soft, dry grass just above the water mark. The cool, clear water lapped against her bare feet, inviting, alluring, demanding.

She stood, slipped quickly out of her shorts and shirt and tossed them to the bank with her towel. She stepped into the water, feeling the coolness slip around her ankles, her knees, her thighs. Kicking off, she swam to the center, her strokes slow and languid, unhurried. She dipped her face into the water, then her hair. Floating on her back, she watched the moon and the clouds, and she waited.

Would he come?

The lovely, liquid movement of the river heightened her senses. She had never been so aware of her own needs, her own passion—a passion so strong and so hot that it hadn't burned out in ten years. Ann let her eyes drift closed as flutters of anticipation rippled through her.

Would he come?

She stood in the chest-high water, letting the coolness lap against her breasts. The water gliding across her skin made the fire inside her burn deeper, deeper for Drew.

Would he come?

Suddenly he was there, on the bank, waiting for her. And the yearning grew stronger, a powerful, undeniable ache throbbing inside her as she stood without breath, watching him for an endless moment. The time had come.

Slowly, as if in a dream, she moved toward him, feeling air touch first her shoulders, then her breasts, her stomach, her thighs, her legs. And each part of her was vividly awakened by the knowledge of what was about to happen with Drew. Finally with Drew.

Slowly she stepped from the water and into the waiting warmth of his arms. He wrapped the towel around her shoulders, pulling her close as he met her eyes in a long, searing gaze.

"I knew you'd come," she whispered, her lips trembling—not with fear or cold, but with deep, deep emotion.

With her hands at the back of his neck, she pulled his head down to hers, immediately capturing his lips. He seemed startled at first by her boldness, then with a groan of pleasure, he kissed her back with reckless abandon. They merged together, desperate, driven, each taking and demanding, each giving and savoring, as ten years of waiting and wanting went into that kiss. Their bodies clung, their souls touched, and the world stopped.

The intensity shattered Drew's control. He squeezed his eyes closed, feeling his arms tremble as he held her tightly to him. Her body was smooth and sleek and quivering against his, her mouth warm and moist and seeking. And he knew if there was a heaven, it had to be here, right now, this moment, holding Angel in his arms after all these years.

"Angel," he murmured, catching his breath, trying to fight the swirling force that threatened to pull him under. "Don't you think we should go back to the house?"

"No." She breathed the words against his lips. "I always dreamed it would be here."

He held her away from him, fixing her with an urgent blue gaze. "This is no dream, honey. This is reality, just you and me, here and now. Are you sure this is what you want?"

She touched his face with her hand, outlined his lips with one searching finger. He caught her hand in his, brought his mouth deliberately to her palm, but his eyes never left hers.

"Don't you think we've waited long enough?" she asked breathlessly, feeling the anticipation start to build all over again as her heart thundered in her chest.

Their gazes clung for a moment, then with an urgent groan, Drew lowered his mouth to brush it across hers, whispering kisses along her neck and shoulders as the fire shot deeper into her veins. His hands on her back pressed her to him, and Ann, arms locked tightly around his neck, stretched her body full length against his in an open, unmistakable invitation.

Aggressive, demanding, his mouth accepted what she offered. Deftly he parted her lips with his own and plunged his tongue deep inside to mate with hers.

Her hands moved over him, stroking, touching, caressing. She wanted to savor, to drown, to lose herself in the waves of desire rolling over her. She slipped her hands beneath his shirt, desperately exploring the heat of his skin. Sensing her need, Drew stepped slightly away, pulled his shirt over his head and flung it aside. The rest of his clothing was unsnapped, unzipped and similarly dispensed with. Ann's breath caught in her throat as he straightened, magnificent in his nakedness and his desire.

They came together again, and for a long moment, stood that way, feeling the marvel of their bodies meeting for the first time.

This is reality, Ann thought. Everything else was a dream, a dim precursor to this moment.

"We're long overdue for this, Angel," he whispered into her ear as he pressed her close.

He kissed her fiercely then, his hands racing over her. He pulled her down beside him on the soft grass, breathing her name over and over again. Her fingers rode over his shoulders and down his chest to his hips, her eyes savoring every revealing detail of his masculinity. The full impact of what was happening overwhelmed her, made her retreat a little inside herself as she lifted her gaze to his. He caught her hand in a warm, reassuring grasp as he lifted her fingers to his lips.

"Don't run away from me," he urged softly. He kissed her tenderly this time, the movement of his lips restrained, patient, waiting for her. His hands roamed over her, lingering here, testing there along their persuasive journey as his gaze enthralled hers with enticing promise.

"Angel." He breathed the words into her neck. "Come with me."

"Where?" she whispered, letting her fingers slide through his hair. She moved against him and tiny points of passion ignited in every part of her.

He cupped both her breasts, touching, caressing and molding her shape to his hands. He tugged gently at the peaks, and the passion exploded inside her.

"Come see heaven with me," he invited, his voice slipping over her like a velvet wing.

His touch was slow, torturous and infinitely tender, letting her know he wouldn't make the trip without her. He slid his hand along her leg, tracing a soft, seductive pattern on the inside of her thigh. Teasing her, taunting her, daring her to let go, his fingers stroked her until she felt the pressure mounting inside her, contracting and releasing to the motion of his hand. Deep and hot and glowing, it grew and grew until she thought she would die from the thrill of it.

The years between them melted. He kissed her deeply, his lips promising her heaven and more. He grabbed her hands and held them at her sides, stilling her movement as he lowered his head, scattering tiny, erotic kisses over her stomach and thighs. Helpless, Ann strained against him, feeling the ache deepen inside her as his lips continued their seeking, finding at last the treasure of their quest.

She tried to move, tried to break free from the exquisite torture, but he held her. Held her until she was hopelessly lost, spinning and diving out of control, her breath coming fast as she gasped his name.

Then suddenly he was over her, smiling down at her as he cradled her head between his hands. "Did you like that, darling?" he murmured, his lips barely brushing against hers.

"Yes! Oh, yes!"

"That was just the beginning." His voice, deep and low and filled with an erotic vow, had the heat pulsing through her even stronger. His touch, hard and knowing, sought to arouse her again. She trembled as his tongue skimmed over her lips, tasting her, persuading her. And then he was inside her, and her stunned cry shocked her at first, then embarrassed her, but Drew smiled down at her, knowingly, tenderly, triumphantly, erasing all thought from her mind as he masterfully guided her toward their ultimate destination. His eyes, gazing down at her, burned with desire as he moved inside of her.

His rhythm slowed, intensely prolonging the journey as he whispered to her, urged her with kisses and caresses until neither of them could wait any longer. She felt the tension heighten as he clutched her to him, his body shuddered as his lips met hers in a thorough, aching kiss. And then, in a burst of joy, in an explosion of sensation, they were there.

Hearts pounding, bodies still joined, they lay together for breathless moments as they slowly, deliciously, floated back to earth.

Drew kissed her once more, tenderly, wonderingly as he shifted his weight from her and settled himself beside her. Propping himself up on one elbow, he gazed down at her and brushed his fingers through her hair. She smiled up at him and he bent quickly to kiss her eyes and then her lips. Her soft sigh broke the silence.

"I hope that wasn't a sigh of disappointment," he said softly.

Her laughter was like the soft tinkle of a wind chime. "Did I act as if I were disappointed?"

"Well, no," Drew admitted, his eyes deep and sensuous as he traced a finger along her jawline. "In fact, you were sensational."

She caught his hand and held it against her cheek. "Really? I mean..." she trailed off, averting her gaze in sudden embarrassment. "I haven't had much experience with...sex. I hope *you* weren't disappointed. I wanted so much to please you," she added shyly.

"Oh, baby," he said on a groan, drawing her into the circle of his arms and holding her close. "If you'd pleased me any more, I think I might have died."

They lay for a long time, shoulders touching, hands locked, as they gazed at the sky. Ann couldn't remember when she had felt so relaxed, so *free,* so unencumbered by anger and jealousy and guilt. Nothing had ever felt so right to her than lying here with Drew.

She breathed deeply, filling her senses with the sweet essence of the river, with the soft flutter of the leaves overhead as the wind drifted through them. From the shadowy depths of the woods, an owl called again, but the sound no longer made her feel lonely.

She lay her head against Drew's shoulder, feeling the steady, reassuring beat of his heart. His arm tightened around her as his lips touched her hair.

"I'd like to ask you something."

"What is it?" she asked lazily, not bothering to rouse from her position.

"Why did you change your name?" His words fell softly into the darkness around them. "I've often wondered about that."

She stroked his chest absently with her fingertips. "I guess I just didn't feel like I deserved it anymore, or wanted it. I'd done some things, thought things, that I was ashamed of and that I knew would have disappointed my father. He always had such expectations of me, and I didn't think I could live up to them anymore."

A trace of bitterness crept into Drew's voice. "I never thought those expectations were fair. He heaped responsibilities on your shoulders that should never have been yours to bear. He never let you be a kid."

And he and Jack and Aiden hadn't been much better, Drew realized with disturbing afterthought. They'd all relied on Angel to keep them out of trouble, pushing their recklessness to the limit knowing she'd be there to bail them out. Not one of them had ever stopped to ask her whether or not she wanted that role. They'd just expected her to do it. She was "Angel."

"I'm sorry," he whispered, his voice jagged with emotion.

She raised her head from his shoulder and turned to look at him. "What for?"

"For making you feel you had to change yourself."

"It wasn't just you," she denied softly. "It was a lot of things. Besides, I always thought Angel was a silly name for a grown woman anyway."

He lifted a hand to push the damp, tangled curls back from her face. "I've never known anyone whose name suited her more."

"Maybe once," she said wistfully. "Not anymore."

"Have you changed so much? I don't think so," Drew said softly. "You're still the most beautiful, caring woman I've ever known. Maybe you've changed, but not in the important ways."

"You've changed, too," Ann said as she gazed down at him with misty eyes. "You're so... sensitive."

"Sensitive?" He growled the word with a mock frown, shaking her lightly, and dispelling as he did their serious mood. "What about virile, masculine, incredibly sexy?"

Ann gave him a slow, daring smile. "You're that, too, but it's your—" She flattened a hand and ran it over his stomach, reveling in a sense of power when his muscles contracted. She dipped her hand lower. "Sensitivity that moves me."

"If it's sensitivity you want, it's sensitivity you'll get," he assured her as he lifted her and pulled her on top of him, letting her feel just exactly what he meant. "Just to prove what a truly liberated man I am, I'll let you be on top this time."

"Your... enlightenment dazzles me," she murmured, stretching out against him and entangling her legs with his.

She touched her finger to the cleft in his chin, then lowered her head and touched her lips to his mouth, lightly at first, a silken caress. Then suddenly, without warning, she thrust her tongue deep inside. She heard Drew's low groan of sensual surprise, and the sound delighted her and filled her with her own bold confidence.

Her hands grabbed his, holding him still, mimicking his earlier movement. She lingered for a moment at his lips, then slowly, deliberately, she moved downward, sliding against the pulsing heat of his body; downward, her lips skimming across the hardness of his chest, playing briefly at each male nipple; downward, her tongue tracing hot, wet patterns around his navel, teasing and nipping his flesh; downward...

He sucked his breath in sharply as he gasped her name. He tore his hands free from her hold and plunged them into her hair. "Angel..."

She lifted her head, her lips curving into a slow, seductive, thoroughly satisfied smile. "Just to prove what a truly liberated woman I am..."

Ten

"I don't suppose you're going to invite me back to the house to spend the night?" Drew asked hopefully as he sat on the ground tying his shoelaces. The first large drops of rain pelting against bare skin had sent them scurrying into their clothes. The wind had picked up, too. It rustled through the leaves, carrying the scent of the rain.

Ann bent down to drop a kiss in his hair. "You suppose right. One step at a time, okay? This has been a very eventful evening for me. I still can't quite believe it happened. For so many years I've had all these negative feelings for you, and now... this." She shrugged helplessly, finding herself suddenly at a loss. She slipped into her sandals and reached down to fasten them, but Drew's hand closed over hers. Adeptly, he dealt with the buckles, then slid his hand up her leg, encircling her calf.

"Are you saying you still hate me?" he asked softly.

In spite of herself, she thrilled to his touch along her bare skin. She gazed down at him, letting her eyes reveal the confusion of a thousand different emotions. "I never hated you, Drew, although I tried very hard to convince myself that I did. That was part of the problem, you see. I always felt so guilty, wanting you when you belonged to Aiden."

"I never belonged to Aiden." Abruptly his hand dropped from her leg. He got to his feet and stood staring down at her, his eyes deep and intense, as though he expected her to challenge him. "She and I should never have been together. It was always you."

"But you married *her,*" Ann said in a voice that was hardly more than a desperate whisper.

"Because I thought I'd lost you forever," he said in a sudden burst of exasperation. "I explained all that to you and I thought you understood. You left. You ran away. I had no idea where you were, and Aiden—well, Aiden was Aiden. She convinced me the child she carried was mine. I had a responsibility to her. Or so I thought."

"What does that mean?" Ann asked, frowning.

He hesitated for a moment as if trying to resolve some inner conflict. Finally he mumbled, "Nothing," then turned away from her for a moment, rubbing the back of his neck with his hand. "Ann—can't we put all that behind us now? Especially after tonight? It was so long ago. You and I still have something very special, and I don't want to lose it."

Ann shook her head sadly as she turned to stare at the river. "You can't expect the past just to disappear because we made love, Drew. What happened ten years ago will always be with us. Tonight hasn't changed that."

"And you still haven't forgiven me, have you?" He ran a weary hand through his hair, then dropped his hand limply to his side. "I don't know what else I can do."

She winced at the open bitterness of his words and the helpless frustration that she knew would hurt him most of all. She turned to face him, her hand reaching automatically for his. She brought his fingers to her lips as her eyes searched his face. "You can give me time. Is that asking too much?"

His face immediately softened and his other hand came up and wrapped around the back of her neck, his fingers weaving through the thick curtain of her hair. "No." His smile was tender. "I'll give you all the time in the world, Angel. I've waited all these years to be with you—sometimes I get a little impatient. Just don't give up on us." His tone was light, almost teasing, and Ann knew that he was trying to dispel the dark cloud that had suddenly formed over the evening. She wasn't sure it could be done quite so easily.

"So we have a few problems. They're not insurmountable," he insisted as he pulled her toward him with gentle but firm pressure against her neck. "I won't let them be. As far as the past is concerned, we can't change it. We can't go back. All we can do is accept it."

They stood holding each other for a long moment in silent affirmation of the special bond between them. That bond had not been severed, even after years of pain and anger and resentment.

A strong gust of wind swept across the water, delivering the rain in its wake. They broke apart, laughing as the drops splattered against their skin and beat with a steady plop against the surface of the river.

"We've waited too long," Ann said, closing one eye as she looked up into the night sky. A raindrop splashed across her nose and she laughed again. There was something exhilarating about the wind and the rain, something primitive and timeless. Like making love with Drew had been, she thought with a catch in her heart. It was emotion at its most basic, as elemental as the rain, and just as cleansing. For one glorious moment she bathed in the sweet, secret joy of it.

"My God, you're so beautiful," Drew murmured, gazing down at her in wonder. "So very beautiful."

She could see rain shimmering in his hair. She ran her fingers through the soft strands, sending the droplets flying. "And you're getting soaked," she said, her smile as soft and misty as the night.

He grinned lopsidedly. "So are you. But you can't expect me to leave when you're smiling at me like that."

She widened her eyes. "Like what?"

"Like we just made love and it was as good for you as it was for me. Do you have any idea how much I want you?"

The blatant sensuality of his voice in her ear sent a quiver of delight dancing inside her. She laughed throatily, her hands clasping behind his neck. "You just had me."

"I want you again," he murmured against her lips, touching his mouth lightly to hers. His hands slid beneath her T-shirt to caress the warm, satin skin along her spine. "I don't think I'll ever get enough of you."

She touched his face with her fingertips, feeling the slightly roughened stubble of his beard. She had never before been so stunningly aware of the differences between the two sexes. Everything about Drew was so virile, so boldly and consummately male. And because of that, she was even more attuned to the subtleties of her own femininity.

"Sure I can't change your mind about spending the night?" His hands moved up and down her sides, grazing her breasts. Ann closed her eyes at the sensation. Soon he'd probably have her begging him to stay.

"One step at a time, remember?" She pulled slightly away, twisting from his arms. He held her for a moment, then let her go.

"For now," he said with a tiny inclination of his head. "I suppose we'd better be on our way before the downpour starts. Will I see you tomorrow?"

"The council meeting is tomorrow night, remember?"

"I hadn't forgotten. Maybe I should come over beforehand and try a little more persuasion?"

Ann knew that he was kidding, but she didn't find it funny. Her brows drew together in a scowl. "What happened tonight hasn't changed my mind about the zoning, Drew. I hope you understand that."

He let out a deep sigh. "Ann, Ann," he said, tapping a finger against her chin. "Do you have to take everything so seriously? I was kidding."

"I know," she said, drawing slightly away from him. "But I just want everything to be clear between us."

"I can separate my professional concerns from my personal ones. I hope you can, too."

She sighed wistfully. "I hope so, too, Drew. But it seems to me in both cases, I stand to lose a great deal more than you."

"That's where you're wrong," he said softly. "But neither of us have to lose. Ann..." He hesitated as he caught her hand, holding it warmly between both of his. "Whatever the outcome of the vote, tonight will always be special to me. Try not to forget that."

"I'll try."

"Good night, Angel." Their hands clung, and then he was gone, quickly swallowed up by the rain-filled night.

The torrent hit just as Ann reached the edge of her yard. With a shriek of dismay, she splashed across the wet grass and leaped toward the dryness of her porch.

She stood for a moment, gazing out into her front yard, watching the constant hammer of the rain against the canopy of oak leaves. The yard and house were completely dark except for the gaslight at the end of the driveway. It cast an eerie, yellow glow into the shadows of the yard, highlighting the flattened beds of flowers. The mingling scent of roses and honeysuckle and jasmine, vividly stirred by the rain, clung as thick and sweet as honey in the rain-drenched night air. In the distance, she heard Drew's car engine start up. She turned her head toward the sound as a soft smile touched her lips.

Regrets? She bit her lip in silent contemplation. Not yet, she decided. Perhaps they would come later. Now all she felt was a deep sense of fulfillment. She felt...? She hesitated a moment, frowning. Was it love she felt? Did she love Drew again? Still?

No. The denial was instant if not confident. It wasn't love. It couldn't be love.

What then? Lust? She couldn't deny the powerful physical attraction that pulled her to Drew. Her stomach gave an odd little somersault at the mere thought of him. Her heart missed a few beats at the memory of his touch, his smile. But making love with him was one thing; being in love quite another. That usually required a commitment and trust, and Ann wasn't at all sure she would ever be capable of either. And yet, even as she dismissed the possibility so abruptly, she felt a small quiver of joy, of anticipation. And that scared her to death.

Love? No. *No.*

As if in final dismissal of the question, she turned to go inside, slipping out of her wet shoes and kicking them aside. She closed the heavy wooden door behind her and automatically twisted the lock as her other hand sought the light switch. But the room remained in darkness when she flipped the switch. Vainly, she flicked it several more times, then with a muttered oath, groped her way down the hall to the kitchen and her cache of candles and matches.

Three matches later, the wick finally caught. Carefully, she picked up the candle and sheltered the flame with her hand. The kitchen appliances cast giant, distorted shadows against the wall and ceiling as she started toward the door, wondering ironically why candlelight could look so romantic at dinner and so spooky in a darkened house.

Making the rounds on the lower level, Ann closed windows and mopped up puddles from the floor where the rain had blown in. Then she went upstairs to repeat the procedure, shoving down the casement window in her bedroom and dabbing at the moisture in the creme-colored carpet with several dry, fluffy towels.

Retrieving the candle from the windowsill, she placed it on the dresser. Her reflection, pale and ghostly in the dancing light, startled her and sent her pulse racing. With a self-admonishing laugh, she began to towel dry her hair.

Her movements halted as her eyes were drawn to the candle. The flame leaped wildly, as though touched by a breeze, and yet she knew all the doors and windows were closed to the night.

She drew in a sharp breath as her heart vaulted to her throat. She could feel an almost infinitesimal coolness, a draft, as if somewhere in the house a door or window had been opened.

With trembling fingers to her lips, she waited silently. Deliberately she inhaled another long breath of air. The hair at the back of her neck prickled with awareness. Some vague, indefinable scent clung to the air, disturbing the unique essence of her private space. *As though someone had been in her room.* Slowly she turned from the mirror, her eyes warily scanning the room. Her closet door was ajar. Had she left it open earlier?

Her hand clapped to her mouth to hold back the scream, Ann whirled and dashed for the door. Instinct and fear propelled her through the black hallway, down the stairs, across the corridor. Her breath came in gasping sobs as she struggled with the bolt on the heavy front door. Finally it gave way, and she threw open the door. The scream came then as a looming, dark figure stood between her and freedom.

She screamed again and tried to spin away, but strong hands held her in a relentless grasp.

"Ann? What's wrong? What happened?"

The deep timbre of Drew's voice penetrated her terror-stricken brain, and she collapsed against his chest, burying her face in his shoulder. He pulled her trembling body into his arms and held her for a brief moment before he gently pushed her away from him.

"What happened?" His voice was calm and commanding, chasing away some of the panic that gripped her so tightly.

A shudder racked her body. Her teeth were chattering so badly she couldn't force words past them, only ragged gasps of breath.

"Some...one's in here. Up...stairs."

They were standing in the doorway and at her words, Drew's head turned to the stairs. "Wait for me on the porch," he whispered against her ear.

"Drew—"

He silenced her with a finger to his lips as he gently pushed her through the door. Then he disappeared inside the house, and for the first time Ann noticed the heavy, metal flashlight he gripped in one hand.

Struggling for control, Ann melted into the deep shadows of the porch. The steady beat of the rain through the trees obliterated every other sound and sent her already jagged nerves to a dangerous edge. Shivering, she hugged her arms to her chest as she waited. And waited.

What was keeping him so long? What if he'd been jumped, hurt? What if he was lying inside—

"Angel?"

At the sound of the hushed voice behind her, Ann jumped violently. She whirled, her hand to her heart, as she saw Drew leap with casual ease to the edge of the porch.

In the misty illumination of the gaslight, he looked tall and formidable as he came to stand over her. She could see his features grimly etched in the faint light. "I checked all the rooms and then went out back to look around in the garden. I couldn't find anything. Let's go back inside and get out of this dampness," he said, pulling his fingers through the soaked strands of his hair.

He held the screen door open for her and Ann, by the beam of his flashlight, led the way into the kitchen. While he toweled himself dry, she lit several candles until the room was warm and glowing.

"You didn't see anything at all?" she asked weakly after he had tossed the towel into the utility room.

Drew shook his head, his tone edged with a curious note of hesitation. "The doors and windows were all closed, and none of the screens appeared to have been tampered with. Both the power and the phone are out, but that's probably from the storm." He shrugged helplessly. "I don't know, Ann. Someone could have come in here while you were gone and then was scared away when you came back. Exactly what did you hear?"

Ann's gaze dropped from his. "No-nothing. I mean... I didn't actually hear anything, but someone was in here, Drew. I know it. The candle was flickering like crazy and I could smell—" She stopped short as she saw Drew's attention quicken.

"What? What did you smell?"

Again she hesitated. "I'm... not sure."

"Well, did it smell like a man's cologne or after-shave? Was it cigarette smoke? Liquor? Any of those things?"

She gazed up at him helplessly. "It wasn't anything that I could identify. I could just tell that someone had been in my room. I know that sounds strange, but it's true. Someone was in there." She wrapped her arms around herself, trying to suppress a shiver. "If you hadn't come when you did—"

"But I did," he said in a deep, soothing voice as he reached for her. The contact was warm and reassuring, melting away the last remnants of her panic. "And I'm not leaving you alone tonight."

His determined tone told her an argument would be useless, which was fine with Ann. She wasn't about to give him one. She merely smiled shyly. "Thank you. You do believe me, don't you?"

"Of course I believe you. Something obviously frightened you badly. Maybe in the morning we'll be able to find some answers, but I'm not counting on it. After this rain, any evidence, such as footprints or car tracks, will have been washed away." He gazed down at her, smiling sympathetically. "Let's not worry about that right now. You're still shivering. You need to get out of those wet clothes. Come on, I'll run you a hot bath."

"Drew," she began thoughtfully as she climbed the stairs behind him. Both of them carried candles, and the leaping shadows along the wall gave a strange, dreamlike quality to the scene. "What made you come back here?"

He glanced over his shoulder, grinning sheepishly. "I ran off the road. My car's stuck. I hiked over here to call a tow truck."

"In the middle of the night? In Crossfield? You've lived in the city too long," she teased gently.

"You're probably right about that," he said with a strange edge to his voice. He opened the bathroom door and stepped inside, placing his candle on the vanity. He took Ann's candle and set it among the bottles of shampoo and bath oil and moisturizer on the ledge at one end of the tub. Turning on the taps, he adjusted the temperature of the water, then picked up one of the bottles at the end of the tub and held it to the candle to read the label.

"Honeysuckle?"

"That's fine," Ann replied. There was a strange, breathless quality to her voice that she found most disturbing. But not as disturbing as the intimacy of Drew's presence in her bathroom or the casual way he perched on the edge of her tub as he ran her bath and almost proprietorially selected the scent of her bath oil.

He dipped his hand in the tub, and a cloud of delicate fragrance rose from the steamy water, drifting between them like a sweet, fragile memory. That same scent had always reminded Ann of warm summer evenings and star-blazed skies and Drew's soft whispers. No matter where she was or how many years had passed, the smell of honeysuckle had always brought Drew back to her.

"All set. I'll get out of here and give you some privacy. I'm going downstairs to have another look around." At her sudden look of concern, he planted a light kiss on her forehead. "It's all right now, Ann. You're safe. I won't let anything happen to you. Trust me."

The door closed softly behind him, and Ann stood for a moment staring pensively at the door. She did feel safe. And she realized suddenly that she did trust him. She trusted him with her life.

Then why not her heart? she wondered sadly as she peeled off her wet clothing and stepped into the tub.

She sank to her chin in the fragrant water that was neither too hot nor too cold, but perfect, just the way she liked it. As though he ran a woman's bath often, Ann thought. And for all she knew, he did. Jealousy stabbed through her with stinging accuracy. Jealousy for the women Drew had known during the years that were lost to her.

She soaked for several minutes, letting the water soothe and relax her until it grew tepid. She climbed out of the tub and reached for a towel. Wrapping it securely around her damp hair, she reached for another to dry her body. Her pink silk robe hung on a peg on the door. She retrieved it and belted it around her before stepping into the hallway.

The door to her bedroom was open, and Ann could see the soft glow of candlelight inside. Drew had brought up at least half a dozen more candles, and had placed them strategically around the room so that even the deepest corners were illuminated. She was touched that he had taken the time and care to try to chase away her ghosts.

"Ann?"

She spun around at his voice, and the towel wrapping her hair slipped free. The long, thick cascade fell almost to her waist, a flaming cloud in the flickering light of the candles. Drew stood in the doorway, his breath in his throat, as they gazed at each other across the room. Ann's eyes slipped over his face, across his bare shoulders, downward to where he'd knotted a towel around his waist. And everywhere her gaze touched him, he felt a nerve in his body jump with awareness. She glanced back up at his face.

He shrugged uncomfortably. "I took a shower downstairs. I hope you don't mind. My clothes were soaked so I hung them up in the bathroom to dry."

"I...don't mind."

His hand was still on the doorknob. He turned to go. "I'll be right across the hall if you need me."

"Drew?"

He turned, his eyes questioning.

"I need you."

Their eyes melted together and Drew felt the almost painful response of his body. He crossed the room in two strides, drawing her to him as he breathed in the scent of her. He buried his face in her neck, savoring the taste and the feel of her. Ann's head tipped back in sensuous response.

His hands found the belt of her robe and quickly unknotted it. He pushed the soft fabric from her shoulders and it whispered to the floor, the shimmering pool a subtle complement to the creamy texture of her legs. Drew felt his heart thrash against his chest as her fingers found the edge of the towel and tugged. And before the terry-cloth had joined the silk on the floor, she was back in his arms.

He lifted her off the floor until she was over him, gazing down at him. Her hands plunged into the deep gold strands of his hair as her lips sought his in a kiss that seemed endless and utterly fulfilling. She wrapped her legs around him, pressing against him, and Drew groaned deeply into her mouth. He shifted her slightly, pulling her even more tightly against him in just the right place. His body threatened to explode at the intense sensation.

"Now," she pleaded against his lips. "I need you so—"

Drew moved toward the bed, staggering slightly. Not from her weight—that was nothing. But from the sheer force of the passion raging inside him. They fell to the bed, arms and legs wantonly intertwined as they lay face to face. His lips swept over her face, his hands raced over her skin, hot and searching.

"Can you feel how much I want you?" He kissed her eyes and her lips and her throat. "I've ached for you for so long. And now that I've had you, the need is a thousand times stronger."

She answered him with a long, searing kiss that left them both gasping. He lifted one of her legs and wrapped it over his hip. With one quick move, he plunged deeply inside her. He paused, savoring the exquisite torture before he began to move, slowly at first, then faster, more urgently. He whispered to her, his voice thick and dark, as he encouraged and suggested and promised. Their moans mingled. Ann's head was thrown back, her eyes tightly closed as her body began to shudder and tighten around him. Drew felt his own body responding, felt a powerful, headlong rush toward the edge. And then he was over and crashing back to earth as he fought for breath.

Afterward, they lay back against the softly scented sheets, listening to the beat of the rain against the windows, occasionally murmuring softly to one another before they fell into a sleep that was deep and content.

Angel? Angel?

Ann's head thrashed against the pillow as she tried to move away from the relentless weight holding her down. She was suffocating, but the harder she fought, the more resistant the iron band became.

Angel! You're with Drew, aren't you? How could you? Your own sister's husband.

Go away, Aiden. Leave me alone.

I'm not going away, Angel. I'm never going away. And you'll never have Drew. He's mine, Angel. He'll always be mine. Do you hear me, Angel? Angel?

"Angel? Wake up, Angel."

At the sound of the deep voice beside her, Ann's eyes flew open and she bolted upright in bed. She stared blindly into the candlelit room for a moment, her eyes unable to focus. Then slowly the horror returned. She turned her tormented gaze to Drew. He was sitting up in bed, staring at her, his blue eyes filled with concern. He was so close she could reach out and touch him, feel his warmth, but it was only an illusion. In reality, he was a million miles away from her.

"She was here, Drew."

Eleven

A cold chill crawled up Drew's spine at the look in Angel's eyes. Fear, despair, horror—he saw all that in the beat of a heart as he gazed into those haunted green depths.

Automatically he reached for her as he murmured soothingly, "It was just a nightmare, darling. You're safe." God, she felt so cold, he thought in panic. Now that the storm was over, it was stifling inside her bedroom but her skin was cold and damp and pale, as though she'd been locked away from the sunlight for a very long time. "Angel? Are you all right?"

"She was here. I heard her."

"Who was here?"

"Aiden."

He stared at her silently for a moment, the breath knocked from his lungs. The skin at the back of his neck tingled with dread. What was she saying...she couldn't possibly mean...

"It was just a bad dream," he said quickly. "A nightmare."

Ann shook her head slowly, her eyes wide and dark against the whiteness of her skin. "She was here, Drew. She knows about us—"

"Angel, don't. Don't do this." With a savage jerk that was more from panic than anger, he hauled her against him, his arms wrapping around her as though he could protect her, shield her from anything—or anyone—who tried to keep them apart. But she was stiff and cold in his arms. She lay against him, unresistant, but he had the terrible suspicion that she had somehow managed to slip away from him again.

He closed his eyes and held her, willing her back to him. Lying back against the pillows, he cradled her, soothed her hair with deliberate restraint.

"Ann, listen to me. You had a dream. A nightmare, and no wonder. You were badly frightened earlier. But everything's all right now. I'm here, and I'll take care of you. Just don't pull away from me."

She lay silent for a long moment, but Drew could feel her body slowly begin to relax against his as he continued to talk to her.

"It seemed so real," she whispered at last, her words muffled against his chest.

"I know, honey, but it wasn't." He kept his tone even and low as his hand continued to stroke her hair. "Aiden's dead, Angel. She can't come between us anymore."

He felt her chest rise and fall in a deep sigh.

"I know. But I can't forget her, Drew. No matter what she did, she was still my sister and I...just wish...I wish I'd been able to forgive her before it was too late. When I think of all the time I wasted, all the jealousy and hate and resentment I harbored for so long—" She shuddered, closing her eyes against the pain. "I think all of this—you and me—would be so much easier to accept if only I had forgiven Aiden."

He smoothed the hair back from her face, pausing at the wetness he felt on her cheek. With a start, he realized it was a tear. Angel's tear. He'd never seen her cry before, not one single tear, even when she'd broken their engagement that terrible night. He felt a powerful surge of emotion, more intense than any he had ever known.

When they were younger, he'd always marveled at her strength, and yet even then he'd felt an almost overwhelming need to protect her. That need rocked through him now with the force of an earthquake. An emotion that strong, that consuming, could only be love, and the knowledge moved him, deeply, profoundly. He wanted to share the wonder of it with her.

But not now. Not tonight, when he knew that that one revelation might very well push her farther away from him.

He lay holding her for a long time, until he could tell by the even rhythm of her breathing that she had finally fallen asleep. Gently he slipped from beneath her and laid her head against the pillow. He got up and strode across the room to raise the window, letting in a welcome breeze.

The rain had slackened to a steady drizzle through the trees. The moon shone through patches of low-lying clouds, but the yard below was almost completely in darkness. Drew stood for a moment, arms braced against the window frame as he stared out into the wet blackness.

He'd been so convinced that making love would draw them closer, take them farther away from the past, but it had done just the opposite. He didn't know how to deal with Angel's guilt, her fears, everything that bound her to the past. He didn't know how to make her see that everything that had happened to Aiden she had brought on herself. He had no wish to hurt Angel any more than he already had, but maybe it was time she knew the truth, all of it, about her sister. Maybe that was the only way to make her see that her guilt concerning Aiden was such a needless waste.

She was here, Drew. She knows about us.

Drew's heart froze, as if plunged into a bucket of ice water, at the memory of those whispered words. That one word, that *name,* still had the power to chill him to the bone. The very notion that Aiden could be alive—dear, God, what that would mean—

He closed his eyes at the implication, hearing again her voice, her warning, her last final torment.

I'll give you your divorce, Drew. But don't think that means you can go running back to Angel. You don't want me? Fine. But you'll never have her.

Your threats don't mean anything to me anymore, Aiden. There's nothing more you can do to hurt me.

No? I wouldn't be too sure about that. You go near Angel, and you'll live to regret it. But she won't. Live, that is. Think about that, darling, *while you enjoy your precious freedom.*

Drew plowed his fingers through his hair, remembering and trying to forget. Aiden was dead. She couldn't come between them anymore; it was Angel who kept them apart now. Angel, with her memories and her pain and her misplaced guilt. Beautiful, sweet Angel with her scar that ran deeper than he'd ever imagined.

He turned and crossed the room to the bed, staring down at her still form. The candles had all extinguished themselves except for one or two that sent dark, distorted shadows creeping along the walls and ceiling as the wicks burned lower. He could see her face in the flickering light, her skin smooth, almost translucent, and softly glowing. The russet mist of her hair swirled and floated in long streamers against the white background of the pillow. Her lovely, delicate hands were clasped beneath one side of her face as she lay sleeping with the serenity of a child.

The episode of the dream had been shoved, at least temporarily, aside in her mind, but Drew wasn't so lucky. He stood staring broodingly down at her as his mind twisted and turned like the shadows on the ceiling.

He had waited so long to be with her.

After his divorce from Aiden, when she'd delivered her final blow, he'd resigned himself to the fact that he would never have a life with Angel. After three years of pure hell with Aiden, he knew she didn't make idle threats. And after all that he'd done to Angel, the one thing he couldn't do was risk her life. So he'd tried to make a new life for himself without her, tried to immerse himself in his career. He'd tried to forget about Angel, telling himself that they were not meant to be, that it wouldn't have worked out anyway. But losing her had been a constant torment, like a raw, gaping wound in his soul that had never properly healed. Until tonight, that wound had never completely stopped hurting.

And now there was another threat to their fragile beginning, and he didn't know how in the hell to deal with it. He wanted a future with Angel more than anything, but the past had such a grip on her, he wondered now if he would ever be able to free her. After tonight, he wasn't sure she even wanted to be free. More and more he was coming to realize how Angel relied on those negative memories and emotions to protect herself from him.

He lay back down in bed and wrapped his arms around her, securing her to him. She slept on, but Drew's eyes did not close for a very long time.

Ann floated pleasantly on the delicate balance between sleep and reality. She awoke, then drifted off again. With a reluctant sigh, she finally pushed away the lingering fragments of a dream and opened her eyes. She immediately focused on Drew, and with a startling flash, realized her dream had not been a dream at all. She had finally made love with Drew Maitland, and it had been a beautiful, glorious awakening.

But it hadn't lasted. It couldn't last. The past wouldn't be banished so easily. Hardly had her moment of blissful surrender ended when all the old doubts and insecurities had begun closing in on her, trapping her once more. This man she had once loved so deeply had married her sister.

Fully dressed, he stood at the window staring out, his brows drawn together in a brooding frown. His expression was as bleak and gray as the weather outside, and just as threatening.

Drew's gaze shifted to hers, and found her staring at him. The moment should have been tender and warm, but his grim expression did not change. "Good morning."

"Good morning. You're up early." Warily, she watched him approach the bed.

"I wanted to have another look around downstairs and outside."

Anxiously, she sat up and pulled the sheet around her. "Did you find anything?"

"No." He sat down on the edge of the bed, his eyes never leaving her face. "There was no sign of a forced entry at any of the doors or windows."

"It must have been my imagination," Ann said, not totally convinced. "I feel so silly for overreacting like I did."

"That's not the overreaction that concerns me."

"What do you mean?" She looked at her hands clasped tightly together on top of the sheet, she looked at the watercolor of a lighthouse hanging on the wall opposite her bed. She looked everywhere but at Drew.

"You know exactly what I mean." His voice was low and determined. Ann knew that tone and what it meant. He wouldn't give up until he'd had his say. "I'm talking about the dream you had last night."

"It was just a dream—" She started to move away but his hand streaked out and hooked hers.

"It wasn't just a dream, Ann. It told us both exactly how you were feeling last night after we'd been together. Why do you feel so guilty about making love with me? There's nothing wrong with us being together. Why can't you see that?"

"Because it's so complicated—"

"It's not at all complicated. It's very simple. I want to be with you and I think you want to be with me. Nothing else should matter. I can't help but wonder if you aren't using your guilt and all the other emotional garbage you carry around as a safeguard to keep you from getting too emotionally involved with me. Every time we start to get close, *you* drag it between us. Why? I know I hurt you once, when I was young and stupid and selfish, but isn't it time to put all that behind us?"

She snatched her hand away from his, smarting from his unfair attack. "I can't make all those feelings go away just because I—" Her first instinct had been to say *just because I love you,* but she knew that wasn't possible. Was it?

The silence lengthened until Drew prompted her. "Just because you what?"

"Just because I slept with you," she said lamely. "I can't help the way I feel, and last night didn't change anything."

"Then it must have meant a hell of a lot less to you than it did to me," he said angrily.

"You know what I mean. I don't want to talk about this anymore, Drew. Not this morning. It—hurts." She touched his arm with tentative fingers but he shrugged them off.

"Does it?" His voice was cold and bitter. "I'll tell you what hurts me. Holding you, making love to you, and then realizing, when it's all said and done, that you'll never let it go any further than that."

"That's not true. You promised me last night you'd give me time—"

"You've had ten years, Ann. Ten long damned years. If you really wanted to be with me, you'd walk out that door with me right now and not look back at this place. I'm willing to do that for you, right now, this minute. We could go anywhere in the world you wanted to and start fresh. But you can't do that, can you? *Can you?*"

She met his eyes for a moment, then dropped her gaze. "No. Because I don't have a right to be with you." The words were whispered into the charged tension of her bedroom.

"What kind of crazy talk is that?" Drew asked, scowling down at her in exasperation.

"It's not crazy," she said defensively. "Everything I've ever wanted I found last night with you. I used to lie awake at night, after you and Aiden were married, wishing that it was me you were holding, me you were loving. I wished for that long and hard with no thought or concern for anyone else. And some of those wishes came true."

"What are you talking about?"

"I wished so hard for things to change so that you and I could be together again. I wished that Aiden—" She broke off as her eyes closed briefly. "When I heard about her miscarriage, do you know what my first reaction was? I thought 'Now he can come back to me.' Do you know what that did to me, when I realized what I'd been thinking? I felt so guilty, like some kind of an unfeeling monster."

"Wishing for something doesn't make it come true," Drew said bitterly. "If it did, you and I would have been together a long time ago. What you felt was a perfectly normal reaction. Beating yourself up over it all these years isn't. Ann, you have to let go of all that—"

"She was my sister!" Ann burst out.

"And your sister was no saint! She didn't deserve this martyrdom you seem intent on forcing upon her." Drew stopped and took a deep breath. When he spoke again, his voice sounded strained, as though he had to work very hard to keep it controlled. "Aiden made her own choices. What happened to her happened because she wanted it to happen, because she made it happen."

He got up and paced the room, his fingers plowing deep ridges in the dark gold of his hair. He spun back around to face her, his expression grim and resolved. "Aiden didn't have a miscarriage, Ann. She had an abortion."

Ann lifted her horrified gaze to his, as if seeking a denial. "I don't believe you," she whispered, her fingers against her lips. "Why would she do that?"

His tone had gone flat, unemotional, as if what he was saying didn't matter at all. Or as if he'd said it before, over and over again in his mind. "I found out several months later. She took great pleasure in telling me that the baby wasn't mine and that she'd tricked me into marrying her. She laughed about it, as though it were a huge joke."

A heavy, ominous silence shrouded the room like a shadow creeping across the light.

"That doesn't make sense," Ann said at last, almost to herself. "Why would she do that? She knew I loved you—"

"That's *why* she did it. You were always blind to a lot of her faults—you and your father both. He claimed she was willful and high-spirited, but what she was was a cold, calculating bi—" He broke off suddenly, as though aware of going too far. He paused for a moment, then looked back at Ann. "Why do you think she always talked you into wearing your hair short? Because her long hair attracted more attention that way. Why do you think she always picked the most flattering colors and fashions to wear for herself, telling you they weren't your style? She couldn't stand for you to get any of the attention, and you let her get away with it. You wore those plain clothes, you cut off your beautiful hair because Aiden expected you to.

"Aiden controlled and manipulated you, Ann, and your father let her. Hell, he was just as bad. He expected you to take care of Aiden, keep her in line when he couldn't or when he didn't want to be bothered with either of you.

You're staying out here in a house that's crumbling around you because *he* laid a guilt trip on you before he died."

"Stop it!" Ann cried, putting her hands to her ears. "You don't know what you're talking about. I wouldn't expect you to understand about loyalty—"

"Loyalty? This isn't loyalty, it's an obsession with you! That's why you refuse to face the truth, and the truth is Aiden used you, she used us both. She did everything she could to keep us apart because she couldn't stand to think of you having something she couldn't have."

"And if you'd really loved me, nothing she said would have kept us apart! The fact remains that you were with her when you professed to love me. Don't put all the blame on her just to ease your conscience or my guilt. That only makes it worse. You and Aiden were divorced seven years before you came back here, Drew. *Seven* years. I can't help but ask myself, why now? Why now and not a year ago, or five years ago?"

His eyes narrowed on her. "What are you saying?"

She took a painful swallow as his eyes chilled her with foreboding. "Your company wants my land. You need my council vote."

He stared at her for a moment as the implication of her words dawned on his face. "Your estimation of me must be pretty low if you could think that," Drew said coldly, pivoting toward the window. His eyes were distant and bleak as he stared out at the dreary sky. "You're never going to let go of the past, are you? You'll never be able to trust me because that one mistake will always be there, undermining whatever we tried to build. I guess there's nothing left to be said."

He turned from the window and strode across the room toward the door.

"Where are you going?" Ann asked fearfully.

He stopped at the door and glared back at her. "I'm leaving. There's no hope for us. You're tearing me apart with your doubts and indecisions, your guilt and your fear. I'm getting out now, before I go crazy trying to make you forget a past you seem to find more fascinating than the future I have to offer you. I want to be with you, Ann, more than anything, but I won't fight this battle every day of my life."

Ann jumped up, wrapping the sheet around her as she faced him, her eyes blazing. "Now who's running?" she taunted. "What did you expect, Drew? That you could just waltz blithely back into my life and everything would be forgotten and forgiven? You think you can claim Aiden tricked you and expect to be excused—"

"Why in God's name do you have to keep bringing *her* into this? I'm getting damned tired of that, Ann. This is between you and me and no one else. I asked you once to come with me. I won't ask you again."

"Oh, an ultimatum now, is it?" Ann said scathingly. "All right, here's one for you. If you walk out that door now, don't ever expect to come back through it."

He turned, his hand still on the knob as he stared at her for a long, silent moment. "Life's for the living, Ann. It's too bad for both of us you can't see that."

Twelve

Go after him! her mind screamed, but her legs refused t obey. Instead she sat down on the bed, weak and trem bling, as she heard the front door slam behind him with a awful, empty note of finality.

So it was over, she thought numbly, pushing back her hai with a shaking hand. The episode was finished. Drew wa gone. She could get back to her nice, safe little life. Sh wouldn't have to think about the past every time she looke into his eyes; she wouldn't have to worry about who he sav every time he looked into hers. She could just get on wit her life, existing day by day, drifting along as though thi interlude had never happened.

She wouldn't have to see his slow smile that sent shiver of sensuality spiraling through her. She wouldn't have to fee the warmth of his arms around her nor the sweet, torment ing pressure of his body against hers. She would never agai have to lay wrapped in the haven of his arms, secure an protected and . . . loved.

She wouldn't cry, she told herself firmly, blinking back the stinging moisture gathering behind her lids. She hadn't cried when her sister died. She hadn't cried in years and years, and she wouldn't do it now. She wouldn't shed one single tear over Drew Maitland. *Angels don't cry,* she reminded herself bitterly, hearing the words spoken in her father's admonishing tones.

But the tears came faster than she could stem them. A storm of emotions, a flood of pent-up feelings, ten years of unshed tears. The sound of her own sobs, breaking the terrible silence of her bedroom, shocked her. She put her fist to her mouth, trying to stifle them, but it was no use. The cloud had burst, and even through her pain, Ann realized how wonderful it felt, cleansing and healing and long, long, overdue.

When the tears were finally spent, she got up from her bed, calm and resolved, as she went into the bathroom to shower and dress. As miserable as she felt, she couldn't stay in bed all day, feeling sorry for herself. She had obligations. People were depending on her, she thought harshly as she brushed her hair vigorously, then twisted it up in its usual knot. She paused for a moment to stare at her reflection. *Why do you think she always talked you into wearing your hair short?*

Beautiful, clever Aiden whom Ann had always admired and adored until that one fateful night. Aiden, who had come between Ann and the man she loved, and had somehow managed to leave Ann carrying the burden of guilt....

She fixed herself a cup of coffee downstairs, then carrying it with her, prowled aimlessly through the house like a prisoner in his cell block. This house, her father's house, was haunted by a thousand memories, and yet that was one of the reasons it was so hard to let go.

Life's for the living, Ann. Like a drum beat, Drew's taunting retort echoed through her mind. Finally, disgusted and distraught, she picked up her briefcase and fled the house, running from her thoughts and her memories.

"Come in, Ann," Viola Pickles invited without a smile. "You're a little early. No one else is here yet."

The screen door closed with a *screak* behind Ann as she stepped into Viola's tiny, redbrick house on Riverside Drive. She followed Viola into the living room and took a seat on the worn olive-green sofa while Viola excused herself to fetch the tea.

Ann's eyes roamed the crowded room with avid curiosity. She'd never been in Viola's home before, had never really given a thought to the dour little woman's existence outside the classroom.

But as Ann gazed around now at the myriad framed photos clustered on every square inch of end tables and chests, at the dozens of identical, crocheted doilies, stiff and white and representing hours and hours of tedious, solitary stitching—it hit her suddenly that Viola Pickles was a lonely woman.

She had no family that Ann was aware of, but judging by the pictures, she must have had at one time. Ann picked up an oval, gilt frame from the table next to her and studied the young couple in the picture.

The man towered over the girl by a least a foot, his black hair sleek and gleaming, his dark eyes intense as he stared at the camera with wary regard. He wore a naval uniform and one arm was draped possessively over his companion's shoulders.

But it was the girl who captured Ann's attention. Her cheeks and lips were hand-tinted a pale pink, while her eyes were a deep, deep blue, almost violet. Only a hint of a smile touched her lips, but there was an air of excitement about her, a subtle, mysterious glow.

Ann looked up from the picture to find Viola staring at her across the room. With a shock, Ann realized that behind those thick glasses, Viola's eyes were deep blue, violet, the eyes of the woman in the photo.

Guiltily, Ann dropped her gaze to the picture in her hands. "I hope you don't mind," she said hastily. "This picture fascinated me. She's—you, isn't she?" Ann asked softly.

Viola set down the tray and came to sit beside Ann on the sofa, taking the photo from her hands.

"It was a long time ago," she said, staring down at the picture, her voice devoid of emotion.

"You made a very handsome couple," Ann said with a smile. "Who was he?"

"His name was Jonathan Albert Wilkerson. He was twenty-one years old when that picture was taken, and I was only seventeen. We'd just gotten married."

Ann's eyes widened in surprise. "I never knew you were married."

"Few people do," Viola admitted hesitantly, as though she were not used to talking about herself. "I'll never forget the day we first met." She blinked twice, as though she was trying to focus, but whether on the past or the present Ann wasn't sure.

"It was August 12, 1943, and it was so hot that day you could see the steam rising from the sidewalks. I was in the front yard of this house—it was my parents' house then—picking the last of the summer roses. I heard someone humming and I looked up to see Johnny strolling down the sidewalk as though he hadn't a care, even though the whole world was at war and he was soon to be shipped out. I remember how blindingly white his uniform looked in the sunlight, and how he stopped dead in his tracks when he saw me.

"It took us both that way," Viola said softly, but her voice was still emotionless, her hands holding the picture steady. "He was stationed in Corpus Christi, and the very next weekend, he came back and we were married. A month later he was sent to Europe and I never saw him again. No one knew we were married, and it was a long time before I found out he'd been killed. A friend of his wrote to me about it. Johnny had told him all about me, he said."

"I'm... sorry," Ann said inadequately, not quite knowing the correct response.

"My parents never found out," Viola continued without acknowledging Ann's words. "I kept my maiden name, I stayed in this house with Mother and Father until they both died. I had nothing to remind me of Johnny except this picture."

Nothing, Ann thought sadly, and yet so much more than that. With a devastating flash of insight, she saw all the long, lonely nights Viola must have spent, all the empty holidays, the birthdays that passed by in a blur as time marched relentlessly onward.

"You never remarried?" Ann asked softly.

"Oh, no. I never even considered it. Besides, I had my memories and my teaching. I've never minded living alone. You and I are a lot alike, I think. You have a fine sense of the past, Ann. I'm glad you're on our side."

Ann sat for a moment without responding, her gaze sweeping over Viola's stern features, the creased mouth that never wore a smile, the deep frown lines across her forehead, the eyes that were without sparkle. Viola may have lived for the past, but it obviously hadn't been a happy existence. Even when she talked about Johnny and the time in her life that must have been happy, there was no longer even a spark. She had lived her life for a memory that no longer even mattered.

And as Ann sat there seeing Viola as if for the first time, she suddenly saw herself, in ten years, then twenty, then thirty, growing older and more bitter with each passing year, and still imprisoned by a past that was only a dim remembrance. *Life's for the living.*

The doorbell rang, drawing Ann from the future back to the present. Viola got up and set the picture down without a second glance as she went to answer the door. Chattering like squirrels, the other ladies of the Historical Society all scurried in, greeting Ann heartily as they found seats.

"Girls, I've got a confession to make," Bernice announced in her booming voice. "I was as dead set against Riverside Development as the rest of you, but I have to tell you, Drew Maitland has won me over and made me see the light. This development project is the best thing that could ever happen to Crossfield. I'm convinced of it." She sat back in her chair, crossed her arms over her healthy bosom and regarded them all with a satisfied smile.

There was stunned silence for a moment, then everyone started talking at once. Viola wrapped her knuckles soundly against a wooden table, bringing the ladies to attention much as she would a classroom of rowdy twelve-year-olds.

"Why this sudden swing?" Viola asked pointedly as she directed her attention to Bernice. "Really, Bernice, you were always one to be taken in by a handsome face."

While Viola bent over the tea tray and poured herself a cup, Bernice leaned toward Wilma, who was sitting next to Ann, and said in a loud whisper, "If that isn't the pot calling the kettle black."

Viola straightened, teacup in hand, her mouth set in a rigid, relentless line. "We can't afford to lose perspective here. Crossfield has always been a nice, comfortable, safe little town. Riverside Development wants to change all that."

"We're stagnating in our own complacency," Bernice retorted, taking two cookies from the tray and handing one to Wilma. "If you'd take the time to listen to Drew, you'd understand exactly what it is he's proposing. Change is happening all around us, girls. If we're not careful, all those noisy, smelly factories springing up along the interstate will move right alongside us without regard to past, present or future. Riverside Development will keep that from happening. Their plan will retain the natural beauty of our town and countryside while bringing in more revenue and more jobs. I'd think twice about it if I were you, Viola. All these houses along Riverside Drive will bring a hefty profit."

"I don't intend to leave this house until the day I die," Viola vowed firmly. "Surely the rest of you don't agree with Bernice. Wilma, what about you?"

Wilma stirred uncomfortably beside Ann, looking first at her and then at Bernice before saying, "Well . . . actually, I do think Drew's plans have merit."

Viola's expression became even more severe. "And the rest of you?" she asked crisply. Several ladies nodded their heads. Viola spun around to Ann and fixed her with a direct glare that had Ann squirming as though she'd been caught passing a note in class. "You haven't changed your mind, I hope. The rezoning vote is tonight. I'm counting on you, Ann."

"Ann's duty is to carry out the wishes of the majority of Crossfield's citizens," Bernice stated firmly. "Not to cater to one stubborn old woman."

"Ladies, please," Ann pleaded, standing up to address the meeting. "My duty as a council member is to always have Crossfield's best interests at heart. I assure you however I decide to vote, that will be the case. Now, if you all will excuse me, I have to go."

A few minutes later Ann walked down to the river and sat on the bank as a thick fog settled over the water. All was silent except for the occasional plop as a frog hopped into the water, the sound magnified against the wall of mist.

Ann could feel the moisture against her face and arms, and she shivered in spite of the warmth of the afternoon. She suddenly felt chilled as she sat there taking a long, hard look at her life for the first time in years, and the mist falling softly against her skin had very little to do with it.

Nothing remained static in this world, she reflected. You either changed with the flow or you got left behind. Some people preferred to be left behind. She had always thought she was one of them. But now looking back on all the long, lonely years of her life, she had to ask herself why she had allowed herself to drift for so long in yesterday's shadow. The answer was painfully simple. Because that had been her only link to Drew. To take that away from her was to take away the only happiness she had ever known.

But Drew was back in her life now, and he was offering her not only the present but also a future. Why was she so afraid to accept it? Why was she still so afraid to let go of the past? Aiden and her father were dead. Her obligations to them were over. She had obligations to no one now except to herself. And perhaps to Drew.

The plain and simple truth was that she was scared to love Drew again, scared to trust him again, scared she would be hurt by him again, but that fear suddenly seemed a dim thing in comparison with the years and years of dragging loneliness she had glimpsed at Viola's. If she wanted Drew, she had to be willing to pay the price, and the price was giving up the past.

She just had to make sure, for both their sakes, she was ready to do that.

It was late in the day when Ann finally walked back to the house. It was already growing dark because of the fog, and the gaslight at the end of her drive had automatically turned on. The thick haze curled like smoke in the indistinct, yellow glow. Ann stood on the porch for a moment, letting memories swirl like the mist around her.

She and Aiden playing on the swings underneath the old oak tree in the backyard, laughing and squealing as they soared high enough to touch their toes to the leaves. Her father sitting in his study after dinner, head bent over his desk as he worked on his accounts...

Those memories and a million others were so much a part of this old place, and yet looking at it now, Ann felt herself a stranger here, as though she'd just stepped from a time warp and no longer belonged. Or maybe it was because she was finally ready to let go.

She walked into the house, flipping on the light to ward off the early darkness. The message light shone on her answering machine. She dashed across the room hoping it would be Drew, but when she replayed the tape, it was Jack's voice she heard.

She dialed his home number first, and getting no answer dialed his office. He answered on the first ring, as though he'd been sitting there waiting for her call.

"What the devil went on out there last night?" he asked without preamble when she had identified herself.

Ann paused briefly, frowning into the receiver. "What do you mean?"

"I mean Drew left here a few minutes ago after dropping quite a bombshell on me. He said he'd spent the night out at the farm last night because you thought someone had tried to break into your house. Is that true?"

"Well, yes," Ann hedged, not wanting to reveal too much. "I'm sure it was my imagination, though. It's nothing for you to worry about."

But she could hear the concern in his voice when he said, "Ann, Drew was in a very strange mood. He asked me a lot of questions about... Aiden."

Ann felt a sinking sensation in the pit of her stomach. "What about Aiden?"

There was another slight hesitation before Jack continued. "About how she died, about the last time I saw her alive. Ann, what's going on with you two? Have you decided to sell Riverside Development your land?"

"Let's just say I'm contemplating my options."

"But I thought...well, I just assumed when he said he was leaving town after the council meeting tonight—"

Ann's heart stopped. "Leaving town? He said that?"

"Yes. He said he was going to have Riverside send someone else down here."

"Jack, are you sure about this? I mean... he's really leaving?" She knew her voice held an edge of desperation but she couldn't help it. She couldn't let him leave, not without telling him her decision. "Did he say where he was going after he left you?"

"He didn't say. Why?"

"I've got to find him, Jack. I have to talk to him."

There was a slight pause, then, "So it's that way, is it?"

She closed her eyes briefly, whispering, "Yes," as though just admitting it to herself for the first time, too.

"Even after everything he did to you?" Jack asked in a strangely detached tone.

"The past is finally over," Ann said, feeling relief flood through her as she voiced the words. "I don't want to live there anymore."

"You may have a hard time convincing Drew of that. He seemed pretty down when I saw him earlier."

"There's a way," Ann said with new determination. "But I need your help. I need a favor and a big one. I want you to draw up papers donating the farm to the city for use as a park facility, and I want to have them ready for the town council meeting tonight."

"You can't be serious."

"I've never been more serious in my life. It's the perfect solution. Will you do it?"

"What time's the meeting?"

"Eight o'clock. I know that doesn't leave you much time," Ann said worriedly.

"No, not much," Jack agreed. "But I'll do what I have to do."

Thirteen

Ann glanced at her watch, then hurriedly attached tiny pearl earrings to her lobes. She had just enough time to swing by Jack's office for the papers before the council meeting started. She wondered if she should give him a call, make sure they were ready for her—

The overhead light dimmed and flickered, then went out all together, as though the bulb had shot. With an impatient sigh, Ann felt her way across the room to the lamp beside her bed and twisted the switch. Nothing. The electricity was out again.

"Great," she muttered, trying to acclimate herself to the darkness. The fog outside completely obscured the moon. The room was pitch black.

She groped for the top drawer of her bedside table, opened it and retrieved a candle and matches. The wick sputtered, then flared, sending black shadows scurrying toward the corners of the room. Setting the candle on the edge of the dresser, Ann picked up the phone to call the electric company, but the line was dead.

If she'd had any second thoughts about getting rid of the farm, Ann decided she didn't now. The inconveniences were becoming more and more difficult to live with—

Her thoughts broke off as a sound interrupted them. She stood dead still, listening. There it was again! A sort of muffled rustling noise, as if someone was moving softly about somewhere in the house.

A tremor of warning shot through her, and with it came an awareness of something dark and sinister. An almost overwhelming sense of danger swept through her. It was more than just fear; it was as though she had a direct connection with the source of the danger.

She picked up the candle and stepped tentatively across the room. The hinges squeaked, sounding as loud as a scream as she pulled back the door. She paused, listening, lifting the candle in her hand and peering down the hallway.

All was silent. The rustling had stopped. Probably nothing more than a tree limb against a window, she decided, trying to shake off the persistent sense of danger. But the feeling was so prevalent, it was almost tangible, like a heavy, black cloak dropping over her shoulders.

Almost with a will of their own, her eyes strayed down the hall to the closed door of Aiden's room. And as she did so, another indistinct sound came to her from behind the door.

Ann's first instinct was to run, but something held her back, some remnant of rationale that told her her imagination was running away with her. She took another step toward Aiden's room, and her hand reached for the knob.

The door swung silently inward. Ann held the candle tightly in her grasp as her eyes frantically searched the shadowy corners, then, more slowly, her gaze roamed the room. There was a slight movement on the other side, as though a stray breeze had stirred the air, leaving behind a strangely familiar scent, spicy, exotic. *Shalimar*...

The cloak of danger tightened around her, almost strangling her with its insistence. Fear pulsed through Ann with every beat of her heart as she hovered in the doorway.

"Aiden?" The name was a whisper as Ann's throat tightened on a scream.

Something moved in the shadows. Ann's gaze clung to the darkened corner by Aiden's bed. Slowly, deliberately, a distinct form materialized and separated from the blackness, moving into the center of the room. Candlelight softly touched each familiar feature....

Drew glanced at his watch as he pulled into the parking lot at Jack's office. He was supposed to be at city hall in fifteen minutes for a pre-council meeting with the mayor, but halfway there he'd discovered he'd left his briefcase in Jack's office and there were papers in it he had to take back to Dallas with him tonight. Papers he'd hand over to his replacement, he thought with a grimace as he opened the car door and got out.

Driving through town earlier, after he'd left Ann at the farm, he'd had the perverse notion that he'd buy the whole damned town, bulldoze the place to the ground, and take away her comfortable, little hiding place.

Because that's exactly what it was, damn it, whether she admitted it or not. The farm, the town, her job—all made a nice, safe little place for her to watch the world go by. But as much as he wanted to, he realized he couldn't force her out of the past. She had to want to come willingly.

And that's why he was going back to Dallas tonight. He wanted to inform his superiors that he was removing himself from the project. Whatever the outcome of the meeting tonight, he wanted no part of the project any longer. He wanted a resolution between him and Ann without anything—or anyone—clouding the issue. He just hoped she'd be willing to give him another chance.

He sighed deeply as he ran a tired hand across his eyes. He'd never seen her angrier than she had been this morning when he'd left, but how could he blame her? He must have sounded like the worst kind of heel, lashing out against Aiden as he had, trying to sugarcoat his own betrayal. He'd never meant to tell Ann about her sister. He'd never wanted her to know the truth, but he'd been desperate, and now he'd pushed her even farther away.

The very worst thing he could have done was attack her family. Drew didn't begin to understand all the complexities of Ann's loyalty to her father and to Aiden; he only knew that he'd give anything to have her feel that way about him.

Jack's secretary, Kate, looked up and smiled as Drew tapped on the glass door. She got up from her desk and came to unlock the door for him.

"Jack's got you burning the midnight oil, I see," Drew said as he stepped inside.

Kate threw a glance heavenward. "A last-minute emergency. He went out to grab us some dinner. I'm surprised to see you back here so soon."

"I left my briefcase in Jack's office. All right if I get it?"

"Sure, let me unlock the door for you. Jack always keeps everything locked up tighter than a drum around here."

"I'm sure his clients appreciate that," Drew said, throwing her another grateful smile as he entered Jack's office and flipped on the light. "Mind if I use the phone while I'm here?"

"No problem," Kate assured him as she closed the door behind her. Within seconds Drew heard the muted clatter of her typewriter as she settled back down to work.

His briefcase was lying on the floor in front of Jack's desk where he had left it earlier. He picked it up and set it down beside him as he perched on the edge of the desk to place his call. By the time he finished talking to Mayor Sikes, he was running more than a few minutes late. With a muttered oath, he hurriedly stood as he grabbed the handle of his briefcase and yanked it up. The corner of his case caught a leather folder lying on Jack's desk and sent it flying to the floor. The jolt knocked lose the clasp, and the contents sailed helter-skelter.

"Damn it!" Drew slammed his briefcase back down on the desk, then bent to retrieve the folder. Everything seemed to be working against him getting to that meeting on time and seeing Ann, telling her his plans. His whole damn future was at stake, and he was down on his hands and knees picking up Jack's schedule and phone messages.

He gathered up the loose sheets of paper and pink message slips, then picked up the leather planner to stick them inside. An envelope slipped out of the pocket on the inside cover and fell to the floor. With another oath, Drew picked it up and started to shove it back inside. His movements froze as he stared down at the envelope in his hand.

He would have recognized that handwriting anywhere. After the divorce, it had gotten so bad that he'd hated to check his mail, dreaded to see that flowing, flowery script that invariably signaled a new threat, a new promise, a new plea in the letter inside.

The postmark was smudged, as though something liquid had been dropped on it and rubbed off. The letter might have been years old, but something inside Drew set off a warning, maybe because his thoughts had been so tuned to Aiden since his and Ann's quarrel. Maybe because Ann's dream had brought back too vividly that final ultimatum. *If you go near Angel, you'll live to regret it. But she won't.*

Numbly, he removed the single sheet of paper from the envelope and unfolded it, scanning the words quickly with a terrible premonition of dread. "Dear Jackie. I'm writing to make you an offer you can't refuse...."

"Oh, my God," Drew breathed, feeling nausea rise to his throat as he quickly finished the letter. Everything was so clear now—the shots in the woods, someone in Ann's house. It all made sense now. The past had been more threatening than he could ever have imagined. While he'd wasted time arguing with Ann, her life had been in danger. Was still in danger—

He stood quickly and grabbed for the phone. "Is Ann there?" he almost shouted when one of the council members finally picked up the phone at city hall.

"She's not here yet. Is that you, Drew? Where the hell are you two—"

Drew hung up the phone and quickly dialed the number of the farm. He let it ring ten times before slamming down the receiver. Kate looked up in surprise as Jack's office door opened so abruptly it was flung back against the wall.

"Call Sheriff Hayden and have him meet me at Ann Lowell's place!" Drew shouted, already pushing open the front door.

"What?"

"Just do it!" The glass door slammed closed with a bang. Drew was already backing out of the parking space by the time a stunned Kate had picked up the phone.

Inside Jack's office, a draft of wind caught Aiden's letter. For a moment, the sheet of paper hung suspended in the air. And then slowly it fluttered to the floor....

Ann stood motionless in the doorway of her sister's bedroom, her breath trapped in her throat, stifling the scream that still clung there.

"What's the matter, Ann?" her cousin asked in a voice that was at once familiar and strange and fraught with a dark, hidden emotion. "You look as if you've seen a ghost."

For a moment Ann could only stare back at him, feeling relief flood through her. She put a hand to her heart as she let out a long breath. "Jack? What are you trying to do—scare me half to death? What are you doing in here?"

He stepped forward slowly, moving to Aiden's dressing table. He picked up the glass swan jewelry box and held it up, observing the delicate sculpture almost abstractedly. "I've been thinking about Aiden all day," he said softly. His features were shadowed by the candle glow, but when he looked up at her, Ann thought she saw sorrow in his eyes. Sorrow and something else, something that might have been pity.

"What are you doing here?" she asked again, trying to assuage the lingering unease. "Did you bring the papers?"

"Papers?" His gaze dropped to the crystal jewelry box as he turned it in his hand, watching the candlelight spark the edge of the glass.

As Ann stood watching him, the scene began to waver, as though the flickering light played tricks on her vision. She blinked once, then again, but all she could see was darkness, as though she were deep, deep underwater. She could feel the cold seeping through her skin, touching her very soul. And terror—terror everywhere—

She was struggling with someone, someone who wanted to kill her. She could feel the weight of the water closing over her head as hands around her neck pushed her deeper, deeper. She fought her way to the surface, gasping and clawing at those relentless hands. For one brief moment air touched her face and flooded into her lungs. Moonlight showed starkly across a face she knew so well....

Then she was plunged downward again, pushed farther and farther away from the light—

Jack's face swam back into focus as he stood there staring at her, still holding the glass swan in his hands. He took a slow step toward her, shifting the glass from one hand to the other, as if testing its weight.

Run, Angel!

Where the silent command came from, Ann never thought to question. She whirled, still clutching the candle like a beacon as she headed for the stairs.

She was already on the landing when she felt Jack's hand catch her arm. Ann swung around, her momentum throwing them both off balance. The candle flew from her hand as they both tumbled to the floor in complete darkness. Ann heard the muted clank of the glass swan hitting the thick rug beside her head. Then Jack was on top of her, holding her defenseless with his weight as his hands closed around her neck.

"Don't make me do this," he begged as she clawed at his hands with her nails. "Don't make me do it the hard way."

"Why?" She gasped the word into the darkness as her fingers still tore at his grasp. Her mind screamed a denial even as she felt his fingers tighten around her. "Why did you kill her?"

She couldn't see his face, but his voice was filled with the same pity she had glimpsed in his eyes. She understood why now. He was sorry, but he was going to kill her, too.

His grasp loosened slightly as he stared down at her in the darkness. "I thought it would be so easy. I'd talk you into selling the farm, take what money I needed and you'd never miss it. You never missed your trust fund, but Aiden did. It's funny, isn't it? Uncle Adam gave me control of yours and Aiden's money because he didn't trust Aiden. And Aiden didn't trust me. Of course, she needed the money as desperately as I did. That's how she found out it was gone."

He was talking to her quickly, in the same defensive tone he'd used as an adolescent to explain away whatever trouble he happened to be in at the moment. For some reason it seemed important to him that she understand why he was about to kill her. Ann lay silently, waiting for his grasp to slacken still more. She let her arms fall limply to her sides. But her heart thrashed wildly in her chest, and her mind raged against him for what he had done to Aiden and for what he was about to do to her.

"She was blackmailing me, Ann. She found out I'd embezzled the trust funds, and she was going to send me to prison if I didn't pay her back, with interest. I couldn't get my hands on that kind of money. Not just like that. And there was no way I could go to prison. I wouldn't last a day there. What else could I do? It was her or me."

Ann could feel his eyes on her, even in the darkness, and knew what he was thinking. Now it was him . . . or her.

"You could have come to me for help," she whispered desperately.

"I needed money, not a lecture," Jack said, his tone suddenly sounding angry. "You would have condemned me without so much as a blink. That's why I decided to try to scare you into selling the land. It might have worked, too. You were scared last night, weren't you? But I never considered you might want to *give* away the land. Lord, Ann, what were you thinking? This place is worth a fortune. . . ."

As he talked on and on, Ann realized what he was doing. He was prolonging the inevitable. He wasn't murdering her for the enjoyment of it. Quite the contrary. She really believed he had genuine feelings for her. But Jack had always put himself first. Why hadn't she realized that before?

Her hand moved silently across the carpet, instinctively searching for a weapon where one would not likely be. Her fingers touched something cool and hard—the glass swan jewelry box. Her heart leaped to her throat as her fingers closed around the crystal.

"I can't wait any longer, Ann," he said sadly. "Kate's expecting me back at the office. Would you do me a favor? Would you please close your eyes—"

With one lightning move, Ann's arm swung upward. The darkness gave her attack the element of surprise. Jack barely had time to duck, but the glass swan still caught him solidly at the temple. With a moan of pain, he fell sideways, his hands slipping from her neck.

Ann scrambled away, using arms and legs to struggle to her feet. Groping for the banister, she started down the stairs. The air thickened with smoke. Ann could only imagine that the flung candle lay smoldering somewhere below, but she couldn't take the time to find it. She had to get out of the house now!

She heard a noise behind her just as a hand clamped around her ankle. For a moment she teetered on the top stair, arms flailing at the air. Then, as if in slow motion, she toppled downward. Only Jack's grip around her ankle kept her from tumbling down the stairs. Gasping and panting, she struck out with her other foot and caught him in the face. With a grunted curse, he released her and she was suddenly free.

Half rolling, half crawling, she was halfway down the stairs before she got to her feet. She took the rest of the steps on instinct alone, flew across the corridor and pulled open the heavy wooden door. Breathless and terrified, she fled into the night.

Her car stood in the drive, but her keys were upstairs in her purse. She rushed toward Jack's car and opened the door, feeling frantically for the ignition. He'd taken his keys!

For an eternity it seemed, Ann contemplated her choices: the road to the highway and pray for a car to come along, or the old River Road and across the bridge to Sam McCauley's place. She was almost sure Jack would expect her to take the highway. With the instincts of a trapped animal, Ann whirled and headed blindly, desperately, toward the river.

The fog thickened as she neared the water. Gray swirls of mist rose from the water, hiding the edge of the bluff. Slipping and sliding along the top of the mossy bank, she followed the raging, rain-swollen river toward the road. Sam

McCauley's property lay just beyond the bridge. If she could cross it, she could reach help.

And suddenly there it was, soaring above her, rising out of the mist-shrouded river. Ann crouched there for a moment, shaken and terrified as she listened to the sounds of the night. Was Jack out there somewhere, listening for her?

"There're only two ways to go, Ann." The disembodied voice floated through the haze, chilling Ann to the bone. He'd somehow guessed where she'd go, and had followed her. She lifted her head, trying to gauge the direction. "You can go across the bridge, or you can come back this way. Which will it be?"

With trembling legs Ann began the nightmarish ascent up the road to the bridge. The wooden planks groaned beneath her weight as she stepped onto the bridge. Water dripped from the rusted rafters overhead. The surging of blood in her temples echoed the rush of the water three stories below her. The rotting floor beneath her feet vibrated with the sound. She took another step, feeling one of the boards shift and give. She drew back her foot.

"I don't think you can cross it, Ann. You were always terrified of that bridge. Come on back down here. It'll be so much easier this way. Why torture yourself?"

She was amazed at how calm his voice sounded, as though he was dealing with a petulant child. Ann moved slightly to her left, and took another step. The wood was solid here. She took a deep breath and continued. One step at a time, she told herself firmly. She wouldn't allow herself to listen to Jack's coaxing voice, rising out of the mist somewhere behind her. She only wanted to concentrate on one step at a time.

She was halfway across when the floor of the bridge disappeared. With a scream, Ann crashed downward, downward toward the swirling, rushing water far below.

* * *

Drew cursed the fog that shielded his view as he sped along the highway toward the farm. Oh, God, why hadn't he seen it earlier? He'd lived with Aiden long enough, he should have recognized the signs, the *desperation.* Maybe he had and just hadn't wanted to believe it was happening again.

In hindsight the clues were all there—Jack's urging Ann to sell her land, the gambling—all seeming so innocent on the surface, but Drew, of all people, should have seen beneath to the darkness that drove him.

He should have seen, but he hadn't, Drew thought, his hands clenching tightly around the steering wheel. And now what if he was too late to stop him? What if—

Don't think about that, he ordered himself. Just a few more miles to go. Concentrate on the road.

But he couldn't stop thinking about the letter, Aiden's letter, and the implication of its contents. She had found out that Jack had embezzled her and Ann's trust funds, and she'd been blackmailing him, threatening to send him to prison if he didn't come up with all the money he owed her and a lot more besides.

She had told him to meet her in Mexico the day before she'd disappeared. It didn't take much to imagine the ensuing scenario. Jack's desperation and Aiden knowing all the right buttons to push him right over the edge. The next step would have been inevitable—with Angel out of the way, he stood to gain it all.

Drew automatically slowed for the turnoff to the farm, but still drove past it and had to backtrack, throwing the car down the narrow lane at a dangerous speed. Visibility was almost zero, but as he rounded the last bend, the fog took on a strangely surrealistic glow.

"Oh, my God." Drew ground the car to a halt in the drive, staring through the windshield in disbelief. Flames shot through the windows of the farmhouse. He lunged from the car, his mind barely noting the presence of both

Ann's and Jack's cars in the the drive. He rushed toward the inferno, his mind screaming a denial even as he felt the heat blasting his face.

He was at the front door, ready to plunge into those flames, when a distant scream slashed like a deadly knife through the darkness. Without a pause, Drew was running toward the sound, each breath a silent prayer.

Ann's fingers slipped a little more as she frantically clutched the wet, rotting wood of the bridge. She could feel the spray from the rushing water below where it pounded against the rocks soaking her legs and clothes, chilling her as she clung to her flimsy support.

"Did you fall, Ann?"

The voice swirled around her, dark and treacherous like the night, closing in on her. Ann had been hidden by the thick haze until now, but her scream had given away her location. Even now she could see the mist frothing at the end of the bridge, where Jack moved toward her.

Ann's arms screamed with pain as she closed her eyes, fighting for strength. Every second was agony, but still she fought. From a distance, another voice pierced the blackness. Ann let out a little sob as she recognized Drew's voice.

"Ann! Where are you?"

She took a deep breath, summoning up the strength to answer him. "Drew!" Her voice was no more than a croak that was quickly swallowed up by the roar of the river.

But Jack had heard her. A gust of wind swept across the bridge, clearing the fog. She could see Jack clearly as he stood looking at her. For a moment their eyes clashed as he slowly started toward her. Ann's fingers slipped closer to the edge—

"Don't do it, Jack!" Drew called from the end of the bridge. "I saw the letter." He moved toward them with an appalling disregard for his safety, quickly traversing the rumbling boards of the bridge as he continued. "I know verything."

Jack paused for a moment, as if torn by indecision. Drew vas rapidly closing the distance between them. As if gaugng the distance, or perhaps his chances, Jack's gaze went rom Ann to Drew then back again. As he stood looking lown at her, he grinned suddenly and shrugged.

"My timing was always lousy. Believe it or not, I'm alnost relieved." Then with a rush of movement, he swept by er and was swallowed up by the fog.

The pounding of his footsteps against the wooden planks choed hollowly against the night. The footfalls ceased, lotted out by the loud crash of rotting boards breaking way beneath a weight. For one split second, all was silent, nd then Jack's stunned cry split the night as his body urled downward to the rocks waiting below.

Ann was only dimly aware of Drew kneeling beside her on he bridge. His powerful hands locked over her wrists. "I've ot you. Let go and I'll pull you up."

Her fingers were gripped like vises around the edge of the vood. Ann looked down at the swirling mist below her. 'I...can't."

"Angel, trust me."

She closed her eyes and loosened her grip. Within seconds Drew was holding her so closely she could scarcely reathe.

She tried to pull away and move toward the rail. 'Jack—" she said desperately.

"Don't," Drew said, his hands gripping her arms. "Don't ook. There's nothing we can do."

She collapsed against him, clinging to him for support as e kissed her in an intense, desperate, out-of-control way hat somehow seemed a part of the tragic, terror-filled night.

"I love you, I love you, I love you," she whispered over nd over again as he lifted her up and carried her across the ridge to safety.

"I told you not to come across that bridge again," she said weakly, still clinging to his warmth.

She heard the smile in his voice. "It seemed the shortest way home this time."

"You risked your life to save mine," she said softly, reverently.

"What else could I do? My life wouldn't have been worth much without you." He kissed her again, tenderly this time and Ann leaned into him, feeling his strength flow into her.

The wind had steadily picked up, blowing the fog upward and away. The western horizon was suddenly alive with color and sound. A flush of orange crept skyward as a siren screamed through the darkness.

Drew's arms tightened around Ann as she struggled to free herself. "Oh, my God," she whispered urgently as realization hit her. "The house is on fire!" With a spurt of energy, she broke from his hold and was running down the path, unmindful of the treacherous footing or of Drew's hand gripping her arm, steadying her, keeping her from falling.

She sprang from the woods just as the roof of the house collapsed, shooting flames and sparks skyward, like an erupting volcano. Two fire trucks were on the scene, and a dozen or so men scurried around the yard, spewing water onto the blaze. But the fire was relentless, tearing down walls, devouring every inch until nothing remained but a smoldering, empty shell of memories.

As if in a daze, Ann watched the last vestiges of her past crumble away. Behind her, a sleek, gray cat crept out of the woods and hobbled toward her on three legs, the green eyes alive with curiosity. Sinking to the ground, Ann stroked the soft fur as she spoke to Watson, softly, soothingly, while the past tumbled down around her.

She didn't even notice that Drew was no longer at her side until she saw him talking to Sheriff Hayden. When he returned, she struggled to her feet, and Watson scurried back to the shadows. "Jack—"

Drew shrugged. "A search party's being organized. There's not much that can be done until daylight, though. I'm sorry, Ann. I'm sorry about everything."

"I don't feel anything," she said woodenly, hugging her arms across her chest as if to reassure herself she was still alive. "It's all gone, and I don't feel anything."

"You will. You're in shock now."

"I believed in all the wrong things. In all the wrong people," Ann said quietly. "I feel like I've been wandering around lost for such a long time."

With one last look at the smoldering ruins of the house, Ann turned and looked up at Drew. In the glow of the dying fire, she could see the lines deeply etched across his face. He looked indescribably weary, but his eyes were as soft as starlight and filled with hope and longing and love. So much love.

"Take me home, Drew," she whispered urgently. "I want to go home."

He opened his arms and she walked into them.

Epilogue

Dappled sunlight danced across the carved headstones as a soft breeze whispered through the trees, stirring the late afternoon heat. But it was cool here. Cool and serene. Ann knelt beside Aiden's tombstone and placed a single white rose against the marble, then traced the lettering with her finger.

Overhead a tiny brown sparrow flitted into the thick leaves of an oak, drawing her gaze upward. She watched for a moment as avid black eyes studied her curiously. A slant of light fired the diamonds in her wedding band, flashing a prism against the smooth surface of the marble. The little bird's head cocked as he shifted on the branch.

It was so quiet here. So peaceful. Ann closed her eyes for a moment, letting the sensations flow over her like a ray of soft light. Warmth. Comfort. Happiness. Whether her own feelings or something more, she wasn't sure—she only knew that she felt a deep and abiding contentment she had never before known. It was strange to think that in losing her sister, she had also found her again. She could let go now, without regrets, knowing that she forgave and was forgiven.

"Goodbye, Aiden."

The soft words, spoken aloud, startled the little bird overhead. With a flourish, he streamed into the sky, circling. For a long moment Ann watched until he was lost in the brilliant white light of the sun.

With a deep breath, she stood and turned toward the gate. Outside the shaded cemetery, the sun beat down hot and bright and relentless. And most welcoming. Ann could see the glare against the windshield of Drew's car. Reclining against the front fender, he waited patiently for her.

When he saw her approaching, he stared at her for a moment, then lifted his hand to wave. And to beckon. Ann's stride quickened.

Life is for the living.

* * * * *

SILHOUETTE®
Desire®
MYSTERY
MATES!